WHAT MATTERS

GARRETT LEIGH

PRAISE FOR GARRETT LEIGH

“Emotional and brilliant…”

ALL ABOUT ROMANCE

“Tastefully erotic … more smart than smutty…”

PUBLISHERS WEEKLY

“Powerful and compelling…”

FOREWORD REVIEWS

ONE

"Three hundred pounds a week?" Eddie's voice rose to a horrified shriek. Cold sweat tickled the back of her neck. "But, Daddy—"

Michael Dean's sigh was that of a man who had far bigger things on his mind. "I'm sorry, sweetheart. But you're going to have to sort this out yourself. I've done all I can do. Besides, it won't do you any harm to get a job. You're *twenty-two*, and Lord knows, you'd benefit from a stint in the real world."

Eddie opened her mouth to retort that three years at Milan's top music school had taught her plenty about the real world, as had moving back to London on her own, but her father had hung up.

Stunned, she dropped onto a nearby bench, the weight of the call hitting her like a train. Her father's bankruptcy was no surprise—the Financial Times had been speculating about the demise of his hedge fund for weeks—but it had never occurred to her that the distant chaos of the post-Brexit stock market would affect her life. A *job*? Was he bloody serious?

With uni and concert practice, when on earth did she have time to *work* for a living?

Oh my God, just kill me now.

But no mass murderer was forthcoming, and so she did the next best thing—or, at least, the thing that was as close to a slow, painful death as she could imagine—and rang her so-called boyfriend.

Ian answered on the third ring, the serene silence at his end a telltale sign that her call was interrupting absolutely nothing.

"My dad's gone bust," she said, before he could jump in with a recap of a day he was bound to have spent drinking rhubarb gin at his favourite waterfront bar. "He says he can't pay my tuition and rent next year."

"Next year? You mean in the autumn?"

"I guess so. We didn't really talk dates."

"Oh. So what are you going to do?"

Ian's flat tone held none of the outraged sympathy Eddie needed to hear right now. She stifled a growl and kicked out at an abandoned Lucozade bottle, sending it skittering across the pavement and into the road. "I don't know what I'm going to do. That's why I'm calling you. For help. Daddy says I'll have to get a *job*. Ugh. How the hell am I going to do that?"

"A job?"

"Yes…a job. Though where he thinks I've got time to do that, I don't know. And, even if I did—" Eddie shuddered "—no part time position is going to pay my rent, is it? I don't know what he's thinking."

"Hmm, it does seem a little unreasonable of him. Have you spoken with your mother?"

Eddie snorted. "I don't dare. She's going to be beside

herself with all that's going on. Can you imagine what they're saying about us at the wine club?"

"Not *us*, darling. Listen, you sound a little stressed. Why don't you come over? We can have a drink, I can give you a massage—"

"I need to find a job, remember?" Eddie snapped. "I don't have time for massages, or to be bloody patronised."

Silence. Guilt coloured the edge of Eddie's panic-laced fury. None of this was Ian's fault, even if he was sitting in his penthouse flat, sipping a gin-and-tonic from a crystal glass, and admiring his own achievements without a clue of what Michael Dean's failures meant for Eddie. "I'm sorry," she said. "You're right—I *am* stressed. Maybe a massage would do me good."

"Of course it would," Ian agreed heartily. "Besides, there's nothing you can do about your little crisis tonight. A massage is just what you need."

Eddie's phone chirped, alerting her to the fact that she'd neglected to charge it before she'd come out. "I guess so."

"I *know* so. Trust me, Eddie."

Eddie's phone died mere moments after she agreed to get a cab to Ian's Greenwich apartment—a cab that would cost a tenner she didn't have in her purse, and the cabbies around Vauxhall rarely carried payment machines.

Grumbling, she found the nearest ATM and jammed in her platinum credit card. For a moment, her PIN number escaped her, and blankness numbed her from the inside out, washing over her. But the respite was brief. Her PIN number was her father's birthday, and as she punched it in, the first feelings of betrayal swept over her. *He knew this was coming. Why did he leave it so long to tell me? What the hell am I going to do?*

Beyond traipsing to Greenwich and drowning her sorrows in gin and mediocre sex, Eddie had no idea.

***

The cab pulled up in Greenwich. Eddie paid the driver and got out, half hoping that Ian, having absorbed the gravity of her situation in the time it had taken her to get to him, would be waiting for her outside his exclusive block of luxury flats.

Of course, he wasn't. In the year they'd been dating, he'd never once met her outside, or even on the landing, preferring to leave it to the concierge to welcome her inside.

Eddie took the lift to the top floor and knocked on the shiny black door. Ian opened it wearing just a fluffy white towel, his perfect, sculpted torso on full display. Eddie drank him in and reminded herself—not for the first time—how lucky she was to have snagged the most eligible bachelor at Goldsmiths University. Ian Frasier-Smith had no shortage of admirers, but for some inexplicable reason, he'd chosen Eddie to hang off his arm.

Not that she did much hanging if she could help it. Ian's inner circle bored her to tears, and it was only his box seats at the Albert Hall that ever persuaded her to step out with them.

"Eddie!" Ian moved back to let her in, grinning like he'd invited her over for tea and cake. "Come in. Sit down. Let me get you a drink."

He ushered her inside and directed her to his oversized leather couch—a vulgar monstrosity that Eddie despised, especially when he tried to get fruity on it. Seriously. When would he learn that there was nothing sexy about sweaty skin on sticky brown leather?

Never, it seemed, as Ian ditched his towel and sat down

beside Eddie, clutching two over-strong gin-and-tonics. "Now," he murmured in a voice some silly undergrad had probably told him was sexy. "Let's forget all about your horrible day and focus on us."

A nice idea, but as spectacular as Ian appeared in all his naked glory, after twelve months of trying, he'd yet to live up to his killer body. And tonight was no exception, though Eddie welcomed the distraction of his fumbling advances. She let him strip her clothes—her silk dress and stockings, her lacy bra and knickers—and then, when she was naked too, open her legs so he could tease her with his fingers—or at least, try.

In the past, his clumsy probing had driven her half mad—not bad enough to push him away, but irritating enough to set her teeth on edge. Tonight it was almost soothing, and she welcomed the discomfort of his naive touch. He slid his cock inside her...and nothing happened, not a jolt, not a flicker. Nothing to spark the inferno she imagined when her dreams took her to a place that nice girls didn't go.

In a flash of abrupt desperation, she raised her hips to meet Ian's rhythmless thrusts, seeking something, anything, to pull her from the nightmare her day—her *life*—had become in the space of a five minute phone call from her father. But it was no good. Ian's thin dick scraped inside her, a world away from where she wanted it most, and her body screamed out for the pleasure she craved.

"*Ian.*" Eddie groaned, thrashing her head from side to side, frustration taking root in the pit of her stomach. "Ian, please...fuck me."

"Yeah?" Ian dropped his head, his sweat dripping in fat drops over Eddie's bare chest, and drove into her with all the finesse of a woodpecker. "You want it like this? Want me to fuck you hard?"

Please. But, defeated, Eddie kept the rest of her pleas to herself, and as Ian pummelled her along the road to his own selfish climax, let her mind drift back to the tragedy that had driven her to his apartment in the first place.

What the hell am I going to do? Her father had made it clear that after this semester, there was no more money for tuition, rent, clothing and food—and anything else she would need for the remaining two years of her degree. She had little idea of how much her first year of tuition at Goldsmiths had set her father back, and she was almost glad of it. The figure he'd quoted for her rent alone had made her eyes water, and that was paid by the month…at the *end* of the month, which was mere days away. Three hundred pounds a week? Where on earth was she going to find more than a thousand pounds by Friday without hitting up her flatmate for a loan?

Eddie had no clue, and she was no closer to finding out when Ian yelled out and shot his load a little while later. He pressed a wet kiss to her forehead and slithered off her, faffing with the condom like it was an unexploded bomb. Like his own come was the worst thing he'd ever seen.

"I'm zonked," he said with a grin. "That was amazing, eh? Shall we go to bed?"

And that, apparently, was that. Too frazzled to argue, Eddie took his outstretched hand and let him lead her to his giant leather bed—the crass cousin of the ugly couch—and slid in beside him, thankful when he pecked her on the cheek and rolled over to "his" side. His detachment had bothered her once upon a time, but as he quickly fell asleep, she felt nothing but relief.

And emptiness, twinned with a renewed, tired version of

the panic she'd arrived with, because despite a round of Ian's finest, she was no closer to a solution than when she'd arrived.

No orgasm, no money, no future.

Fuck my life.

TWO

Eddie woke with a jump, her heart pounding, her skin sheened with a cold sweat. *Damn.* She sat up sharply, pressing a hand to her chest. A breeze rattled her bones, blown in from the open window, and exhaust fumes—the kind kicked out by London buses—made her feel like retching.

Beside her, Ian lay prone and oblivious, and the sight of him, the memory of his hands on her skin, his cock inside her, turned her stomach. *Oh God.* Her heart beat harder than ever. *What on earth's the matter with me? It's only Ian.* But in the dim light of the early morning, the abrupt realisation that his bed was the last place on earth she wanted to be was so intense that her head spun.

I need to get of here.

She crawled out of bed and tiptoed to the living room to gather her clothes, though the logical part of her brain told her that Ian was unlikely to wake. And then she left the flat, bypassing the lifts, running down each flight of stairs like her life depended on it.

Downstairs, she burst through the entrance doors, sucking

in great gulps of air, and as the oxygen reached her brain and eased the anxiety-laced fog, panic turned to embarrassment, and her cheeks flushed with uncomfortable heat. Thank heavens Ian slept like the dead. *Damn you, Daddy, for turning me into a raving lunatic.*

But even as the errant thought crossed her mind, she knew that throwing blame at her father wasn't fair. She had little knowledge of the inner workings of his company, but she'd heard enough on the rare occasions she'd been home in the last six months to believe that he'd fought tooth and nail to save his ailing hedge fund.

Not that the sudden flash of perspective was much comfort, anymore than were the first drops of rain as they fell from the sky and soaked through her thin silk dress. It would've been the easiest thing in the world to go back inside, rouse the concierge and charm him into letting her back into Ian's flat, but as her pulse slowed to a steady beat, and the prickle of unease faded from her skin, the idea of crawling between Ian's Egyptian cotton sheets filled her with horror.

No.

She couldn't go back. Not now, while her father's troubles were still so raw. She'd deal with Ian later. He'd understand —eventually.

Dodging puddles, she dashed across the road, seeking the shelter of the tall buildings, and heading for the nearest ATM. With chattering teeth, she jabbed in her PIN, but the option to withdraw cash didn't appear on the screen. Instead, an alert flashed and the machine swallowed her card.

Flabbergasted, Eddie stared at the screen, waiting to wake up. For this nightmare to end, and her real life to return. But nothing happened. The machine reset itself, welcoming its next customer, and her daddy-funded credit card was no more.

She didn't dare risk her debit card, not that it would've done her much good. Last time she'd checked, her current account had held the grand total of three pounds fifty, but at the time, with the weight of her father's credit card behind her, the paltry amount had meant nothing.

And now it really was nothing, and the only way back to Vauxhall was to walk.

"What you doing out here, missy? You need a cuppa to warm you up?"

Eddie pushed her damp hair from her face and followed the sound of the rough, eastern European accent. "Excuse me?"

The old man stood in the doorway of what appeared to be a greasy spoon café—*Jimmy's Café*, according to the signage— and looked her up and down. "A morning like this is no good for a lady. I'll get you some tea."

He disappeared briefly and returned with a polystyrene cup. Eddie stared at it, her mind addled with cold, and jumped a mile as he thrust it into her numb hands.

"Take it," he barked. "You shivering on my doorstep is bad for business."

Eddie shuddered harder and took the cup, wondering if she'd been dropped into a parallel universe. The reality of her eight-mile walk from Greenwich had kicked in soon after she'd embarked on it, but then a friendly cabbie had taken pity on her, driving her to the outskirts of Vauxhall on his way home, and refusing to take her Gucci watch as payment. She'd assumed her luck had finally run out when the heavens had opened in earnest as he'd driven away, but apparently there was more than one gallant man in London. "Thank you."

The old man nodded and started to turn around, but as Eddie turned away too, he appeared to think better of it and instead stepped aside. "Come inside and drink it. Eat something until the rain stops."

"Thank you, but I can't," Eddie said, though the scent of grease-laden bacon was oddly exciting, given that she hadn't eaten meat in years. "I have no money, and I need to get home."

"No point going home wet and hungry. Sit yourself down. You'll need no money today."

Despite good fortune carrying her most of the way home, another step in the cold, grey deluge seemed unthinkable. Eddie's tired legs made the decision for her, and she followed the old man inside the café and collapsed at the nearest table. "Thank you," she said. "I won't stay long, I promise."

The old man grunted and disappeared, leaving Eddie to her tea, a dark brew that was strange and sweet and warmed her bones with every tentative sip. *Sure beats a soya latte*, and it probably had less calories too. Winner.

When the tea had gone some way to thawing her numb fingers, Eddie set her sodden suede handbag on the table and emptied it out. Some of her sheet music was ruined, and her empty purse and dead phone were no use to her right now, but her diary had survived and had protected the personalised Visconti pen her father had given her after her A-levels.

She opened the diary and scanned the pages. Most were crammed with lectures and concert rehearsals, but if she could find a job that only needed her at the crack of dawn and last thing at night, she'd be laughing.

Laughing. *Ha.* It was preferable to crying, but right then they felt like one and the same.

A plate of scrambled eggs, mushrooms, and perfectly dark toast appeared in front of her. Eddie blinked, like the food and the wonderful smell was an apparition. She'd have sworn blind that she wasn't hungry, but the fierce growl of her empty stomach said otherwise.

Like he'd read her mind, the old man smiled a little. "Hungry, eh? Eat up, missy."

He turned to leave her alone again, but Eddie grabbed his arm. "Thank you," she said. "There must be something I can do to repay you? I could find some cash and drop it off later? Wash up, or something? At least tell me your name."

Amusement danced in the old man's pale brown eyes. "My name is Mr. Nowak, and you? Wash up in my little café? You're not the type for such hard work. Now eat your breakfast."

Not the type for hard work? Tired rage bloomed in Eddie's gut, and she ate her breakfast with increasingly sharp, stabbing motions. She was grateful for Mr. Nowak's kindness, but his assumption was galling. Not the type? Jesus. Was there an invisible silver spoon jammed in her behind that she couldn't see?

If there was, it was faulty. How else did he think she'd wound up penniless in his crappy café?

She shoved her empty plate away, narrowly avoiding her Prada handbag. It took a moment, but as she eyed the bag, her real leather diary, and her Visconti pen, the proverbial penny finally dropped. With her designer gear spread out on the plastic table, her soggy silk dress, and her ruined Manolo Blahniks, to Mr. Nowak, she probably looked like a half-drowned vapid rich girl who'd forgotten her platinum credit card.

And how wrong was he?

The longer she sat there with a full stomach and an empty purse, the urge to find out only grew. Eddie scanned the café, which by now had a handful of customers, and a sign above a wooden blackboard caught her eye. *Help Wanted,* with a phone number and a note to call Sam Nowak underneath.

Bugger that. I can see him from here. Eddie pushed her chair back with a screech of metal on tile and picked up her plate. She strode to the counter where Mr. Nowak seemed to be cooking enough bacon for a small army. "Thank you for my breakfast. I want to work for you in return."

The mirth in Mr. Nowak's eyes remained. "I told you, missy. I don't need your help."

"Oh, but you do." Eddie turned and pointed to the sign. "It says right there that you're looking for help."

"I'm looking for someone to clean tables, load the dishwasher, and make tea. You want to do that?"

"Yes."

"Really? Because I've got no time for people who don't want to do real work."

"I want to work. I *need* to work."

"Why?"

Eddie gritted her teeth. "Why does anyone work? I need the bloody money."

Mr. Nowak eyed her a moment, then banged two plates of fried breakfast on the countertop, smirking as Eddie jumped. "You want to work? Take these to table four."

He shuffled back to the grill without another word. Eddie stared at the plates like they had horns, and time seemed to slow to an animated crawl as she picked them up and scanned the café, searching for any sign of table four.

There were no numbers on the tables. Pride kept her from asking Mr. Nowak, and so she stepped forward, trying to apply some logical thought to the problem. But logic had never been her strong point. She'd once dropped her tinsel halo in her primary school nativity play. It had landed at her feet, but rather than pick it up, she'd sat on the floor and cried, and not much had changed since.

But she wouldn't cry now—not with Mr. Nowak at her back and her hands full of greasy fried breakfast. She stepped forward, analysing the tables that had customers at them. Most were construction workers and tradesmen, clad in dusty overalls and heavy boots, and were already eating. Only one table had nothing in front of them.

Eddie took a deep breath and carried the plates to the men, who glanced up with interest that was likely more for the steaming food than for her. "Table four?"

They nodded. She set the plates down and in a last second flash of inspiration, grabbed a nearby tray of cutlery and condiments. She placed it carefully on the table and picked up an empty tea mug. "Refill?"

The man nearest her nodded. "Please."

"No problem. Enjoy your meal."

She strode back to the counter and thrust the mug at Mr. Nowak, who appeared to have watched the whole exchange. "He wants more tea. Now can I have that job, or what?"

THREE

An hour later, Eddie finally left the café. Mr. Nowak had agreed to employ her on a trial basis, but not, apparently, in a soggy silk dress.

"Come back tomorrow in something that doesn't cost as much as my car."

Fair enough, though Eddie had no idea what kind of car the old man drove. In fact, she had no idea of much at all, and as she stepped out into the by now bustling Vauxhall street, the high of her small victory with Mr. Nowak abruptly wore off. Yes, she had a job, but without knowing exactly how much money she'd need for the next two years, would a minimum wage job in a greasy spoon café be enough?

Somehow, she doubted it, and the ridiculousness of the last twenty-four hours hit her like a stone. *What on earth am I—*

A shower of dirty water splashed up Eddie's dress as a car threw itself into the parking space beside her. Or rather, it was thrown into the space by the feral hood rat driving it. "Hey!" Eddie banged on the window. "Watch what you're doing!"

The man behind the wheel lowered the window, and

Eddie's temper abruptly cooled as the stupidity of what she'd just done hit home. This was London. You didn't screech at hooded young men in cars, no matter how idiotic their driving.

She backed away from the car, much to the apparent amusement of the man, who abandoned his attempt to communicate through the window and got out, unfolding his tall frame from the driver's seat and coming around the back to stop right in front of Eddie. "You got a problem, missy?"

She'd spent all morning with Mr. Nowak addressing her as "missy" and hadn't batted an eye, but hearing it from a young man in ripped jeans and a tatty hoodie reignited the rage her initial fear of him had quelled. "Missy? I'm not a bloody horse, and yes, I do have a problem. You sprayed water all over me by driving like an arsehole."

The man stared down at her, treating her to a pair of deep brown eyes that were utterly hypnotising. "I wasn't driving like an arsehole. I was just driving. It's not my fault the roads are wet. You shouldn't stand so close to the edge."

"To the edge?" Eddie's voice rose dangerously. "I'm not exactly on a river bank, am I?"

"No? Coulda fooled me." The man winked and turned away and disappeared into the hum of the busy city streets, whistling to himself, Eddie apparently—and instantly —forgotten.

She had half a mind to follow him, but with the fresh shower of dirty water, all she could think of was a hot shower, fluffy towels, and her own bed.

Leaving her rage behind, she admitted defeat and went home. Ten minutes later, she let herself into her ground floor garden flat. Exhausted, she shut the front door behind her, hoping to slip past Martha, her perpetually cheerful flatmate, and fall into bed, crawling under her duvet with a mind to staying there until the real world went away.

"Eddie!"

Damn it. Eddie forced a smile as Martha flitted out of the kitchen, coffee in hand, and not hair out of place, like she'd been up and functioning for hours. She probably had. Martha's tendency to rise early and be in bed by nine was one of the reasons she was such a good flatmate. Close as they were, half the time, Eddie never saw her, which made her appearance now all the harder to bear. "Morning. Sleep well?"

Martha frowned. "It's eight o'clock, Eddie. Ian's woke me at the crack of dawn. Where on earth have you been?"

Ian. Shit. In all the excitement of Jimmy's café, Eddie had forgotten all about him. "What did he say?"

"That you'd turned up all upset at his place, and then left in the middle of the night. He didn't sound too concerned, but I was all for calling the police."

"You didn't, did you?"

"No. Your dad said not to."

"My dad?" Jesus Christ, this just got better. "Who called him?"

"I did. I was worried, Eddie. It's not like you to go off on your own. Is everything okay?"

Martha stepped into Eddie's space, her earnest gaze swimming with the empathy Ian had lacked, and the dam finally broke.

Eddie dropped her bag on the floor and covered her face with her hands. "My dad's bankrupt, Martha. He's lost everything."

Martha gasped and pulled Eddie into a clumsy hug that was everything and nothing that she needed, all at once. "Oh God, Eddie. That's awful. What's he going to do?"

"I don't know," Eddie wailed into Martha's cashmere jumper, "but he called me yesterday to tell me he's cutting me off."

"Cutting you off?"

Sniffing, Eddie raised her head. "Yes. He can't pay my rent anymore, and after this term, he can't pay my tuition either."

Colour drained from Martha's face, and for a moment they simply stared at each other before Martha seemed to snap back to reality. "Right. Go and get changed while I make some hot chocolate. There must be something we can do."

Eddie doubted it, but she'd run out of energy to argue. She drifted to her room and dumped her dress in the washing basket, swapping it for pyjamas and the slippers she usually wore at Christmas. On the floor, her ruined sheet music poked out the top of her handbag. She retrieved it and spread it on her bed— perhaps a futile gesture, but she had to practice Beethoven's Ninth if she had any hope of making the first violin section for this year's summer proms, and time was running out.

Despite Mr. Nowak's breakfast still heavy in her belly, the scent of warm chocolate drew her out of her bedroom. In the living room, she found Martha setting out cocoa and cookies, and Eddie's much-neglected laptop. The sight of it reminded her that she still had her final essay to complete for her sonic arts class, but she silenced that particular crisis for now. *Jesus…one meltdown at a time.*

"Is your dad officially bankrupt?" Martha asked. "Because there's some bursaries you can't apply for unless you have no means of support elsewhere."

"He's cut me off," Eddie said dully. "How much more official do they need?"

A lot more official, apparently, as Eddie discovered when

she and Martha trawled the websites offering student grants and bursaries.

"What about this one?" Martha's tone was hopeful.

Eddie shook her head. "It says my parents need to be 'in receipt of tax credits.' What does that even mean?"

Martha didn't know, and with no answer forthcoming on the website, Eddie shut it down. "I'll have to get a loan. They cover tuition, right?"

"It depends which one you get. All students are entitled to a student loan, but Eddie, the rent on this place is—"

"I know, I know, three hundred quid a week. My dad told me yesterday."

"It's not just that," Martha said. "This place has three bedrooms, remember? A hardship bursary won't pay for that, so we'll have to move if you can't pay the rent."

It was nice of Martha to say "we," but Eddie wasn't convinced. Martha had been born with the same silver spoon that Eddie had, and there was no doubt that her father would plug any gap that Eddie left behind. Besides, they'd rented the garden flat so they could use the tiny box room for practice—Eddie on her Stradivariusus violin, and Martha on her flute and classical guitar. To move to a smaller place and have to use her bedroom was unthinkable. "We can't move. I'll make it work, I promise. I already got a job."

"A job? That's great. Where is it? At the concert hall, or something? I heard they were looking for people."

"It's at, er, a restaurant, actually…early mornings and late nights. It's not much, but it should pay what's left of the rent after the loan comes in."

"*If* you get a loan." Martha's scepticism was clear. "How many hours a week is the job? Are you sure you've got time for it?"

Eddie wasn't sure of anything, but she forced the most care- free smile she could muster and reached for a cookie. "It's about forty hours a week, but the place is quiet. With any luck, I can take my uni work with me and do it while I'm there. Honestly, I think it's all going to be fine. Lots of students work while they study. How hard can it be?"

"I guess you'll find out."

"Indeed." But as Eddie sipped her cocoa and ate her way through Martha's cookies, her mind drifted from her current woes and instead settled on the obnoxious stranger from outside the café—and his molten dark eyes and tight jeans. Even his sneer had been arresting, though it still made Eddie's blood boil.

Animal. I hope I never see him again.

The trouble with hoping was that it was usually based on something that was likely to happen—a sad fact that Eddie discovered when she showed up for her first shift at *Jimmy's Café* the very next morning. "*You?*"

Amused coal-dark eyes twinkled back at her. "Yep. Last time I checked, I was definitely me."

Eddie opened her mouth. Shut it again. It was five-thirty in the morning. She had to be seeing things, because there was no other plausible explanation for the apparition of smug handsomeness standing in the kitchen of Mr. Nowak's café. Damn. In tight jeans and a wrinkled white tee, eyes slightly hooded with the air of someone who'd barely woken up, the git was even more gorgeous than when he'd sprayed water up her legs the previous day. "You shouldn't be here. We're not open yet."

"Oh no? Says who?"

"Says the boss. And the sign. Look. We don't open till six."

"So what are you doing here? Getting a jump start on your bacon fix?"

"No, actually." Eddie smoothed her hair in an effort to appear poised and controlled—a tall order with Mr. Smug smirking down at her. "I work here, and I'm pretty sure Mr. Nowak wouldn't want the local riffraff hanging around his kitchen, so I suggest you leave."

"Mr. Nowak, eh?"

"That's right."

"That's who you work for?"

"Yes." Eddie had a flash of inspiration and remembered the Help Wanted sign. "Sam Nowak, and he'll be here any minute."

"Any minute?"

"Yes."

"Sam Nowak?"

"Yes."

The impostor in the kitchen laughed, and in any other circumstances, in any other man, the sound would've been glorious—deep and rich. "Dear God. Pops promised he'd take someone on, but he never said it would be some prissy rich kid. Jesus Christ. Are you serious?"

Eddie prickled indignantly. "Excuse me?"

The man sighed. "Okay, lady, listen to me. The joke's over. I don't care what you're trying to pull, but I haven't got time for this shit. I've got a kitchen to run. Scram, will ya? While I've still got my sense of humour."

"What?"

"You heard. Get the fuck out."

Eddie had heard all right, but as the words filtered through the hypnotic haze the tall, dark, annoyingly handsome stranger cast on her, they made no sense. "You're telling me to get out?"

"Yes."

"Of *your* kitchen?"

"Yes." Mr. Smug walked past her and out into the café. He jabbed the Help Wanted sign with a long, elegant finger. "My sign, my writing, my name. I run this place, so if you really want to stay and work, you'll be working for *me*. If that's a problem, then sod off. If not, dump your fancy stuff in the staff room and be ready in five."

Eddie threw her least favourite handbag into a battered locker with a satisfying thump, grumbling under her breath. Of all the cafés he could've worked at, it just *had* to be this one, didn't it?

Of course it did. The way her luck had gone the last thirty-six hours, it couldn't have been anywhere else. And that smirk. God, she'd wanted to slap it right off his smug face, even when his humour had morphed into a bored irritation. Especially when that had happened. Sam Nowak was an arrogant arsehole, and he clearly thought Eddie a weak and useless little woman.

Well, she'd show him...at least, she would when *he'd* shown *her* what the hell she was supposed to do.

Resolved, she thrust her coat into the locker and slammed it shut. Then she went back to the café and found Sam oiling the huge flat grill by the service counter. "What do you need me to do?"

Sam glanced over his shoulder. "Still here then?"

"Of course I'm still here," Eddie gritted out. "I work here. Now what do you want me to do?"

"I want you to piss off, but as that's unlikely to happen, you can go round and fill up the sauce bottles."

"The sauce bottles?"

"Yes. Ketchup. HP. It's all in the dry store." "Which is where?"

"Behind you, in the kitchen."

"Oh." Eddie retreated to a door she hadn't noticed until now and retrieved giant bottles of ketchup and HP sauce from a store cupboard. She took them out to the café and eyed the many smaller bottles dotted around. *Right. Fill them up. How hard can that be?*

Not very, as it turned out, if she ignored the half-gallon she spilled on the tables. She was wiping up the last of the mess when Sam appeared at the counter.

"Spill it?"

"Only a bit. No harm done."

"Says you. It ain't your stock."

"Not yours either. It says Artur Nowak above the door. That's not you, is it?"

"No," Sam said steadily. "That's my grandfather. He owns the place, but he's eighty-three. Who do you think does the leg work?"

"Not the point," Eddie said, trying not to crow. "I'm just saying you aren't really the boss. Mr. Nowak is."

"I'm the boss of you," Sam countered. "And I'm the boss when Pops isn't here, which is six mornings out of seven, and most evenings until nine, so either way, I'm still in charge. Are you done with those bottles?"

Eddie's small victory faded like it had never been there at

all. She gathered her giant condiment bottles and nodded. "Yup. What's next?"

"Mushrooms. Follow me."

Sam led Eddie into the kitchen and to a row of brightly coloured chopping boards. "Use the dark green one for mushrooms. Light green for any washed fruit and veg. Same for the knives."

"Bit pernickety, isn't it? Colour coding your knives?"

Sam treated Eddie to a withering glare. "It's the law, actually, smart arse, so do as you're told, unless you want EHO to walk in here and shut us down."

Heat flushed Eddie's cheeks. She turned away from Sam and picked up the nearest dark green-handled knife. "Okay, okay, I was only joking. Do you want me to chop *all* those mushrooms?"

The wide, shallow box next to the technicolour chopping boards held more mushrooms than she'd ever seen. Sam came up behind her and reached over her shoulder. "Not the tiddlers. Anything smaller than these ones, leave 'em whole. Got it?"

It was hard to grasp the concept of anything with Sam leaning over her. In her mind, she'd convinced herself that he likely smelled of stale sweat and cigarettes, and so she was sorely unprepared for the dizzying cloud of clean cotton and gently spiced musk that hit her senses.

Beautiful.

Damn. The sentiment laid root before she could catch it, and for a brief, humiliating moment, it was all she could do to stop herself pressing her face into Sam's neck and breathing deep, greedily absorbing as much of his arresting scent as she could before he inevitably pulled away.

Unless he didn't pull away, and—

"You catching flies in that open gob?"

Eddie jumped. "What?"

Sam dropped the mushroom he'd been holding and straightened up. "For a posh girl, you ain't half fucking gormless. Cut those mushrooms, and then I'll show you the tomatoes. Try not to lop a finger off, eh?"

He returned to his side of the kitchen, leaving Eddie equal parts furious and slightly stunned by the effect he'd had on her. *Arsehole.* She was just tired—half addled with sleep deprivation. And nervous, too. She'd play him at his own game once she got in the swing of things, right?

Wrong. As the morning progressed and the café opened for business, Eddie found herself increasingly out of her depth. Cooking was, apparently, Sam's domain, and at first she was glad of it. Carrying plates to tables was a cinch.

But she was wrong again. With Sam tied to the grill and the huge pots of baked beans and stewed tomatoes, Eddie was responsible for taking orders, money, and preparing hot drinks, on top of keeping the café clean and presentable—a tall ask, when every customer seemed intent on opening as many packets of sugar as possible and emptying them over the tables.

"Why do they do that?" She complained when she caught a rare free moment. "It's disgusting."

Sam kept his eyes trained on the grill. "There are worse things to clear up than a little bit of sugar. You should be here on a weekend when people bring their kids in. Now *that's* mess."

"Will you need me at the weekends?" Eddie's heart sank a little. She'd been hoping to keep her weekends free, allowing her to catch up on all the late night practice she'd miss. "Your grandfather hasn't given me a contract yet."

"A contract?" Sam laughed and flipped a dozen rashers of sizzling bacon. "What do you think this is? A bloody bank, or something? PAYE is as official as we get around here. You're lucky you get a payslip."

"A what?"

"A payslip—oh, never mind. You haven't got a clue what I'm talking about, have you? Is this the first job you've ever had?"

Eddie pursed her lips, unwilling to give an inch. So what if she'd never had a Saturday job like some of the other kids at school? Had never pulled pints in the student union either? That didn't make her less valid than anyone else. "I'm just asking if you need me on Saturdays. It's not a problem, I'd just like to know."

"Saturday morning is our busiest shift. If we need you anytime, it's then, so consider yourself told."

"Fine." Eddie turned on her heel and stalked back out into the café. A scene of devastation greeted her. While she'd been talking to Sam, every table in the café had emptied, leaving piles of dirty plates and mugs that all needed clearing. Brilliant. She'd already dripped grease on her Armani jeans. They were her oldest pair, but still—*fuck my life*.

The café door opened. Three construction workers appeared, and then two more, and then a group of five, all wanting breakfast and a hundred mugs of tea. Eddie took the first group's orders, and Sam appeared at her shoulder

"Clear the tables first," he barked. "Can't feed them if they've got nowhere to sit, can we?"

"So what should I have them do in the meantime?" Eddie hissed through clenched teeth. "Congregate at the till?"

"They'll have to. Maybe next time you'll stay on top of bussing instead of standing around giving me earache."

"What?" Eddie seethed, but Sam was already gone, pushing past her to clear the tables. And of course he did it at lightning speed, coming back with a tray so full that his leanly coiled muscles practically waved at her.

I hate him.

And as the day wore on, the more certain of that fact Eddie became. Sam Nowak was conceited, arrogant, and annoying, and the facts that he was gorgeous and awesome at his job were irrelevant…mostly, because even though she wanted to stab him with a fork, Eddie couldn't help admiring the way he singlehandedly cooked breakfast for half of London, all the while supervising her every mistake, of which there were many.

"Can't you count?" he asked exasperatedly around midmorning. "Why on earth did you write four full English on the ticket when there's clearly only three of them sitting there?"

"I'm a little frazzled," Eddie snapped. "I've been working for five hours without a break. Isn't that illegal?"

"Take a break if you need one, luv. Just stop fucking up. You're costing me money."

"You? Or your grandfather?"

"In our family, it's all the same. There's no rich banker daddy in my lot."

"I don't have a rich father either."

"Right." Sam turned away with a smirk that boiled Eddie's blood.

Enraged, she looked for something to throw, but a customer called her away before she could launch a teapot at the back of Sam Nowak's head. *Smug git. What the hell does he know about my life?*

Everything, apparently, if the snide silver spoon remarks she endured for the rest of the shift were anything to go by.

At midday, he cut her loose. "Go home, Cinders. You're done for the day."

"Cinders?" Eddie finished loading clean mugs on top of the coffee machine. "What's that supposed to mean?"

"Does it matter? You're done. Finished. Go home to your castle."

"You're a dick, you know that?"

Sam smirked. "It's been said before. Are you coming back tomorrow?"

"Do you want me to?"

He shrugged. "I'd rather not tell Pops you've flounced on the first day. He seemed quite taken with you."

"And what about you?"

"Am I taken with you?"

"*No.*" Eddie forced herself to meet Sam's gaze, pretending for all the world that it didn't feel like he could see right through her. "I meant, do you want me to come back? I'd rather not waste my time if you think I'm utterly useless."

"You're not *utterly* useless."

"Fine!" Eddie dumped the last mug on the machine and stalked away, slamming into the staff room and roughly jamming the key into her locker. Bloody Sam Nowak. *I hate him.* And as she gathered her things, it was all too easy to imagine that she'd never see him again, that she could walk out of the café with her head held high, knowing that she'd done her best, and that *he* was the epitome of all that was wrong with the male population of London.

But, of course, she couldn't. She *wouldn't*, because even without the perilous state of her finances, there was no way she was backing down. Sam Nowak believed she would fail, that she wasn't good enough to mop the floor of his crappy café. *More fool him.*

"Do you always talk to yourself?"

For the millionth time that day, Eddie jumped and whirled around to find Sam behind her. "Stop sneaking up on me!"

"I wasn't." Sam took a casual bite of the wonderfully burnt toast in his hand. "I came to ask if you wanted something to eat before you left. We don't do much lunch trade in the week, so I've got time to make you something."

"Why would you do that?"

"Why not? Worked all morning, didn't you? You've gotta be hungry, unless you're on one of those stupid diets. No carbs in daylight or whatever."

He laughed at his own joke, and the desire to punch his beautiful lights out returned full force.

"I'm not hungry, thank you," Eddie said with as much dignity as she could muster while leering at his toast with a watering mouth. "And after watching you sweat over that grill all morning, I wouldn't eat here if you paid me."

"That right?"

"Yes. Goodbye, Sam. I'll see you tomorrow."

"You're coming back, then?"

"Yes."

"Good. Oh, and Eddie?"

"Yes?" Eddie turned on her way past him, trying not to shiver at the way he said her name.

"We *do* pay you to eat, as it goes. You get a meal every shift you work."

Arsehole.

FOUR

Eddie spent the afternoon after her first day at the café trying to recover from the most physical labour she'd endured in years. Apparently hours of brutal violin

practice had done little to toughen her up for the real world, a fact she bitterly accepted as she soaked her aching legs in a steaming hot bath.

The fact that she couldn't get Sam Nowak out of her head didn't help her mood either. His eyes, his cotton-scented skin, even his smug smirk, had her so preoccupied that she didn't notice her hands and feet turning into prunes. *Ugh.* She glared at the offending appendages, imagining Sam's face carved into her wrinkled palms. It went some way to dulling his devastatingly gorgeous eyes, but his devilish smirk remained.

With a sigh, she hauled herself out of the bath and padded back to her bedroom. Her phone rang as she tossed her damp towel on the bed. She wondered if it might be old Mr. Nowak telling her not to come back, that Sam's assessment of her performance had been so bleak that he'd decided not employ her after all. Or perhaps her father—who she was in no mood to talk to— wondering if she'd made it home from yesterday's adventures.

But it wasn't her father, or Mr. Nowak, old or young. It was Ian, and for some reason that seemed worse.

Eddie sat on her bed and took the call. "Hello?"

"Eddie! How are you, darling?"

The cheer in Ian's tone caught her off guard. "Erm…fine, I guess? You?"

"Oh, I'm just grand. Anyway, I was calling to see if you wanted to come for a drink tonight? Some of the crew are meeting at the Vic around eight. They're all dying to see you."

Lies. Ian's vapid friends didn't like Eddie any more than she liked them, but she couldn't deny that, despite her aching legs and the lingering smell of grease in her hair, the idea of returning to the real world—to her world—was more than a little tempting. "I guess I could pop out for a few. Are you picking me up?"

"Actually, I'm coming from Monty's. You can get a cab, can't you?"

Eddie wasn't in the mood to remind him that she was no longer in a position to get a cab anywhere, and so she agreed to meet Ian at the bar and hung up.

After drying her hair and dressing in a black maxi skirt and white camisole, she stepped into her favourite gladiator sandals and headed out to the nearest bus stop. The walk took her past the café. She glanced inside, hoping to get a good idea of the evening trade, so she knew what to expect on her first late shift in a few day's time, but there seemed to be no one about, save a few old men…and Sam, who chose to look up at just the wrong moment.

Embarrassed to be caught staring in, Eddie averted her

gaze, heat flooding her cheeks. She put her head down and kept walk– ing, hoping Sam hadn't seen her.

"Can't stay away, eh?"

Rats. Eddie dug deep for her most pleasant smile and turned around. "I'm just passing."

"So I see. Off anywhere fun?"

"What do you care?"

"That's not very nice."

"Neither are you."

"Touché." Sam grinned, though it wasn't quite the smirk Eddie expected. "I told Pops that you'd be back tomorrow. Not changed your mind, have you?"

"No. Why would I do that?"

Sam shrugged. "Dunno. I guess this just doesn't seem like your kind of place. I thought maybe you'd lost a bet, or something."

"A bet? Are you kidding me? Do you really think I'd slave all day in your café for fun? Do you think I've got nothing better to do?"

"I've no idea what else you do with your life," Sam said mildly…too mildly. "And, to be fair, you didn't work all day. I'm still here, remember?"

Guilt was an emotion Eddie didn't expect to feel when she looked at Sam Nowak, but she couldn't avoid the fact that knowing he'd been working since five-thirty that morning made her feel a little bad. "Do you want me to come in and help you?"

"Help me?"

Eddie shrugged. "Two sets of hands make lighter work, don't they? Or something like that."

Sam's usual smirk softened slightly, making his chiselled features briefly boyish. "That's sweet, but I'll be okay. I've been doing this shit so long I reckon I could do it in my sleep, which is just as well some days."

"Are you tired?" It wasn't the question Eddie had meant to ask, but as she gazed at Sam, she realised that she didn't need a response to know the answer. Sam was a beautiful man—despite the fact that he was an arrogant git—but his killer bones and entrancing gaze couldn't hide the signs of fatigue on his face. "Sorry, that was rude of me."

"Was it?"

"Yes," Eddie said. "I imagine I'd be the last person you'd tell if you were tired, because it's none of my business, right?"

"If you say so."

"I do—" Eddie stopped as she realised how daft she was beginning to sound. "Anyway, if you don't need me here, I'd better get going. I've got a bus to catch."

Sam's grin widened. "You're getting the bus? Seriously? Or is that toff code for a horse and carriage?"

The perpetual irritation that seemed to be Eddie's constant companion around Sam returned. "I'm not a toff."

"No? You ain't exactly an East-End cockney either, though, are you?"

"Do I need to be?" Eddie put her hands on her hips, her left foot tapping as sudden rage boiled through her. *Damn him.* "You're not cockney either. You're northern, I can hear it in your accent."

"Leeds, born and bred. Can't get much posher then that, eh?" Sam's tone dripped with sarcasm, and the grin that had briefly softened his features was lost to his trademark sneer. "We're immigrants too. That pushes us up the food chain, right?"

"Don't be so bitter," Eddie snapped. "I bet you've never left this country."

Sam said nothing, and for the first time since she'd met him, Eddie sensed victory. Granted, it was a small point, but a point nonetheless, and something told her she'd need all she could get around Sam Nowak.

"Anyway," she said again with as much dignity as she could muster. "I really do have a bus to catch, so I'm going to leave you to it. Will I be seeing you in the morning?"

"I'd imagine so," Sam said flatly. "Well then."

"Well then," Sam repeated.

And still, Eddie didn't step away. "Anyway—"

"You said that twice already."

"Oh, piss off, will you?" Eddie finally exploded. "I only stopped to be polite."

"Thanks for that."

"For goodness sake. You're so *tiresome*." Eddie turned on her heel and stalked away from Sam Nowak for what felt like the thousandth time that day. How was it possible that she'd only just met him?

Eddie knew the moment she walked into the Greenwich bar that agreeing to meet Ian had been a massive mistake. After her hellish day and subsequent run-in with Sam Nowak, she desperately needed to decompress and take stock of the disaster her life had become. A glass—or three—of wine and a sympathetic ear would've been worth coming out for, but Eddie had been halfheartedly dating Ian long enough to know that he'd likely forgotten all about the financial tragedy that had led to her getting a job at Jimmy's Café in the first place. *I shouldn't even bother telling him I've got a job. He'll only be mortified that it's not at Fortnum and Mason, or somewhere.*

"Eddie!"

Ian's jolly bellow rang out across the busy bar. A few faces in the crowd of pressed shirts, loafers, and tweed turned to stare, first at him, and then Eddie. She cringed, though his greeting was far from unusual. Was it possible that he'd overnight become—Sam Nowak aside—the most irritating man on the planet? Or was it her? After all, she was the one whose world had imploded.

Suppressing the urge to run all the way home, Eddie forced a smile and tentatively waved at Ian. She made her way across the bar and joined him just as he was buying a round of drinks.

"White?" he asked.

"Please." Though, for some reason, Eddie fancied a beer. Her legs still ached and her throat was scratchy. A cold beer would've slid down like a dream.

But such a thing was impossible. The ladies in Ian's life didn't drink beer, not even from the pretentious, bulbous glasses it was served in at bars like this one. The large glass of chablis he thrust into her hands would have to do, even though he was bound to have picked one that tasted of pickling vinegar. That's right—for a rich boy whose parents likely had a sommelier on retainer, Ian had *dreadful* taste in wine.

Still, despite tonight's poison being as acrid as she'd feared, Eddie tipped it into her empty stomach, absorbing the resulting giddy recklessness, which in turn made a second glass seem all the more sensible. Halfway through her third, she realised what a terrible mistake she'd made. Head spinning, she excused herself to the bathroom and splashed cold water on her face. As she looked up, she caught sight of her reflection. *Dear God, I look like a zombie.* And with her pale skin and shadowed eyes, it wasn't far from the truth. She combed her fingers through her thick, strawberry-blonde hair, trying to tame it, but it was no good. Her cursory blast of the hair dryer combined with a damp evening had sealed its fate.

The distraction had, however, gone a little way to sobering her up. With a final, rueful glare at the mirror, she returned to Ian's fold at the bar.

He threw his arms around her, drunkenly clutching her to him like she'd been gone for days. "Aren't you having fun? Isn't this fun?"

Eddie looked up at him, wondering how much of her it would take to lie, but one glance at Ian told her that there was no need. His attention was elsewhere—on a tall brunette on the other side of the bar—and Eddie didn't care. She didn't care at all.

And neither, clearly, did Ian. He hadn't asked her why she'd run out on him yesterday morning, or even acknowledged the reason she'd called him that night in the first place. *I'm nothing to him. A trophy, at best.* And what kind of trophy was she now? Forty-eight hours ago, she'd been the daughter of financial shark, Michael Dean, and a musical prodigy. Now she was flat broke and hadn't picked up her violin since she'd found out about her father's bankruptcy, and it wouldn't be long before Ian dropped her like a stone.

Unless you drop him first...

But the anarchist in her head wasn't loud enough, not today, and perhaps not ever. Ian was a symbol of everything she'd lost—privilege and status—and the sight of him, his clammy hand on her shoulder, the scent of his cologne, was choking, *suffocating*, but she couldn't give it up.

Not yet.

FIVE

Eddie…*Eddie*. Wake up. Your alarm's been going off for ages."

"Wha—?" Eddie cracked open a heavy eye and peeled her face from Ian's silk pillowcase. "What time is it?"

"Ten past six."

"What?" Eddie shot bolt upright and instantly regretted it, her state of apparent undress even more abhorrent than the jackhammer having a party in her head. "Oh God, I'm late."

Ian grunted and rolled over, exposing his naked arse.

Eddie shuddered and turned away, and the renewed blast of her alarm shocked her into action. *Shit*. She was late—really fucking late—and if she didn't get moving soon, there'd be no point bothering to show her face at Jimmy's Café ever again.

She rolled from the bed and scrambled around Ian's bedroom, scooping her clothes from the shiny hardwood floor —clothes that couldn't be less suitable for what was left of her shift at the café if she'd tried. In desperation, she snagged one of Ian's Fred Perry polo shirts from a nearby chair. Tucked into her long skirt, it looked ridiculous, but the camisole she'd worn the night before was practically underwear.

Besides, it stank of whisky and Ian's cigar smoke. *Stuff it.* On her way to the front door—after swiping a tenner from Ian's open wallet—she balled the camisole up and dropped it in the bin.

The bus stop in Greenwich was a five minute dash down the road, but the journey itself took forty-five minutes, and it was gone seven by the time Eddie burst into the café.

Sam, rushed off his feet manning the grill and serving at the counter, treated her to a withering glare. "What time do you call this? I was just about to call Pops in to help me."

"I'm so sorry." Eddie hurried behind the counter and dumped her bag by the till. "I overslept."

"You're an hour and a half late," Sam snapped. "That's not oversleeping, it's not giving a shit. I'd about given up on you."

"I said I was sorry. Look, I woke up at six, but I was in Greenwich and it took me an hour to get back."

"You couldn't have called?"

"I don't have your number."

"Shame." Sam cracked three eggs on the grill. "Watch those, will you? I've got tables to clear."

He thrust a spatula into her hand and stormed past her into the café, leaving her to stare at the fast-cooking eggs with a panic that was close in intensity to how she'd felt when her father had called a few days ago. *Watch them do what?* Eddie had no clue, and she approached the grill like it was an incendiary device, poking warily at the sizzling eggs. The whites were solidifying fast and crackling around the edges, but the yolks remained liquid and gloopy. *Should I turn them over?*

Eddie's idea of cooking was a Waitrose ping meal, but a jolt of reckless abandon surged through her just as Sam swept past her with a towering tray of dirty plates. She flipped the eggs.

He nodded curtly. "Good. You can read tickets then."

Can I? Eddie searched for the source of his backhanded compliment and discovered it in the vein of the order tickets Sam had pinned above the grill. *Oh.* She hadn't taken much notice of what he'd done with the tickets she'd handed him the day before.

She read the first one: *full x 2, bubble, easy eggs.*

Easy eggs. She scanned her brain for where she'd heard the phrase before and found herself in New York, ordering breakfast in an upmarket diner with her father on the last business trip she'd tagged along on before she'd gone to Italy. Eggs easy… over easy. Flipped. *Genius, Eddie. Bloody genius.*

With considerable effort, she silenced the sardonic devil on her shoulder, and focussed on the rest of the ticket. A full English comprised of every meat product on the menu, as well as mushrooms, tomatoes, baked beans, and fried potatoes. Eddie had no idea where to start, but thankfully Sam reclaimed his spatula just as panic began to set in for real.

"Go and put your stuff away. I've left something for you by your locker."

"What is it?" Eddie's lateness had put her in the wrong, and clearly cemented her place in Sam's bad books, so she didn't imagine it was anything nice.

In answer, Sam showed her his back. "You'll see, but don't go pissing around in there, yeah? We're behind as it is."

Fair enough. Eddie grabbed her bag and hurried to the staff room. By her locker was a pristine white apron, starched and crisp, with a note in the scrawl she recognised from the order tickets: *to keep your jeans clean.*

An odd warmth filled Eddie's belly, and she found herself suddenly and irrationally cross. Why couldn't Sam have just told her what it was? And why had he given it to her when he quite clearly couldn't care less about the state of her designer jeans?

Perhaps he doesn't want you roaming his café in filthy clothes? But as sensible as that logic was, it didn't seem right. Didn't feel right. And Eddie had no idea why.

And as she stood dazed in the staffroom, her hangover kicking in with blistering force, she came no closer to figuring it out.

She folded the apron a few times so it wouldn't drag on the floor, and tied it around her waist. Back in the café, Sam was serving at the counter. He spared her a brief once-over that did nothing to calm her spinning head, and gave her a curt nod.

"Nice shoes."

Eddie glanced down at her feet. *Oops.* She'd neglected to account for the sandals she'd worn the night before. "You can hardly see them under my skirt."

"I ain't worried what you look like, woman. It's your feet that concern me."

Woman? Is he serious? "What's wrong with my feet?"

"Nothing…yet. Just don't drop anything on them. Wearing those strappy things, you might as well be barefoot."

"Didn't know you cared."

"Don't start."

"Start what?" In spite of her splitting head, Eddie couldn't resist an innocent grin. "Working?"

Sam rolled his eyes and turned his attention—not that Eddie had ever truly had it—back to the grill. "Throw some plates through the dishwasher, then get out on the floor and clean up."

And so that's what she did, though she quickly learned that

the steamy, soap-scented dishwasher was the last place she wanted to put her face while she was hungover. Shame the customers that kept arriving didn't care. And neither, it seemed, did Sam, if his amusement when he found Eddie at the back door some time later, hot and clammy, was anything to go by.

"Don't tell me you're still half pissed?"

"It's hot in there," Eddie snapped, fanning her face with her hand. "I'm not *drunk*."

"Not anymore, at least. Good night, was it?"

"Can't remember," Eddie admitted before she remembered who she was talking to. She couldn't suppress a shudder, either. She'd left Ian's place in such a hurry that she hadn't had time to shower, and the reality that she'd likely slept with him made her feel even more ill.

So ill, in fact, the world around her tilted slightly. Dizzy, she leaned heavily on the doorframe, sure she would fall, but strong hands suddenly seized her shoulders and lifted her off her feet and deposited her on the back step.

"Sit down," a distant voice said. "Fuck's sake."

The voice was exasperated enough to slowly bring Eddie round. She blinked and found Sam up in her face, glaring at her with an odd mixture of annoyance and concern, and neither emotion sat well with her.

Eddie took a deep breath. Sam raised an eyebrow. "Back with me? Or are you going to chunder on my shoes?"

"Ew. That's hideous." Eddie shoved halfheartedly at Sam's chest. Her hands met warm, solid muscle—leaner and meaner than Ian's—and Sam didn't budge an inch. "Seriously. I'm fine."

"Don't look it," Sam retorted. "Have you eaten today?"

"No. Have you?"

"'Course I have. I'd be on my arse too if I hadn't had my Shreddies."

"Don't make fun of me."

"I'm not." Sam abruptly released Eddie's shoulders and stood. "Not eating is stupid, even without a hangover. Stay there. I'll bring you something."

Eddie opened her mouth to protest, but Sam had already gone. Mourning the loss of his touch, Eddie scrubbed a hand down her face and fished her phone from her pocket. *Shit.* It was gone eleven o'clock and she had a seminar after lunch. Had she told Mr. Nowak Senior that she couldn't work all morning on Thursdays?

Shamefully, she couldn't remember that either.

And it didn't even matter because she hadn't seen Mr. Nowak since he'd hired her, and she very much doubted that Sam would let her leave without a fight, especially as she'd turned up late and hungover on her second ever shift. Which meant she had to steady herself to argue her case, because she couldn't miss this seminar. Her end of year marks depended on it.

Like magic, Sam appeared, a small plate of scrambled eggs and dark toast in hand.

"I can't eat that," Eddie said.

"Try," he countered. "You'll feel better."

"I believe you." Eddie stood carefully. "I meant that I don't have time. I've got to go to uni for a seminar. I think I told your grandfather about it."

Sam frowned, and Eddie steeled herself for a dose of obstinate arsehole, but Sam merely thrust the plate into her hands. "Do what you like, but you ain't leaving this building till you've eaten that."

Eddie made it to her lecture in the nick of time, slipping into the back just as the professor dimmed the lights for his slide show. The presentation should've been fascinating, and the guest lecturer was one she'd looked forward to all year, but as he talked the packed auditorium through the history of contemporary chamber music, Eddie's eyes grew heavy and her neck weak.

Her chin hit her chest and she jumped awake with a gasp, covering her mouth with her hand and darting her gaze around, horrified and embarrassed—two emotions that had been her constant companions for days now. But no one was looking her way, and as hard as she tried to fight it, fatigue overcame her again, helped along by the steadying, nourishing plate of food that Sam had forced on her before he'd let her leave.

Eddie fought sleep, her brain alive with the reality that it was the last thing she was supposed to be doing. Her head bobbed and jerked, and her heart beat too fast, and it seemed like no time at all had passed when Martha slid into the seat beside her.

"Eddie!" she hissed. "What on earth are you doing? Are you all right?"

"Huh?" Eddie jumped, the breakfast Sam had so chivalrously cooked her suddenly in her throat. "What?"

"You fell asleep," Martha said. "The boy beside you was looking at you all funny."

"Oh God." Eddie covered her face with her hands. "Did anyone else see?"

"I'd imagine so. You didn't move when the lights came up."

Brilliant. Kill me now. Eddie sighed noisily. "I'm such a disaster. I needed this lecture to finish my end of year essay, but I've got no notes. What am I going to do?"

"Use mine," Martha said. "Just be careful that you don't copy my words."

Eddie had flat shared with Martha long enough to know how selfless her offer was. Martha was a stickler for fairness, dignity, and rules, and though she was hiding it well, the disapproval of Eddie's current state of chaos had to be killing her. "Thank you. I don't know what I'd do without you."

"Starve, probably, but I have more. I did some research on grants and bursaries. I think you'll be able to get most of your tuition covered if you apply before the end of this term. You'll probably have to top it up with a student loan, and you'll definitely have to pay your own rent, unless we move to a two-bed place—"

"We're not doing that."

"Let me finish," Martha said. "You're going to have to find the rent, which means you'll either have to work forty hours a week all of next term—and every term, until your dad sorts himself out—or you're going to have to work the whole summer and save up some serious dosh."

Dosh. The word didn't sound right in Martha's Berkshire accent, and Eddie smiled wanly, even though Martha's verdict effectively put an end to the summer of sun, sea, and concerts she'd had planned. "Thank you for researching all that for me. I didn't know where to start."

"I know, and it seemed like you didn't have time, especially with the hours you're working. Honestly, Eddie. You look exhausted."

Eddie bit her lip and looked away, unwilling to admit that most of her fatigue stemmed from the night she'd spent on the chablis. Because, honestly? Martha had been the sole sympathetic voice she'd heard all week, and she wasn't quite ready to give it up. "I'm okay, Ma. Really. I've just been a bit… over– whelmed, I guess, not knowing how I was going to stay at uni, but your help has changed all that. I feel so much better now."

And it was true. Eddie's hangover was still alive and kicking—with the added bonus of a healthy dose of humiliation at nearly fainting at Sam Nowak's feet—but her pounding head really did feel clearer, like the light at the end of the tunnel was a blessing, and not a train coming to mow her down and obliterate what was left of her life.

All she had to do now was make it home without falling asleep anywhere else untoward—a task that would have to wait until she'd picked up her replacement sheet music from the library.

After a brief freshen up in the ladies, Eddie trudged to the library. Replacing the music that had been ruined the last time she'd done the walk of shame from Ian's place cost seven pounds that she scraped together from the tips Sam had given her before she'd left the café. And for the first time she could recall, handing over her cash felt like the worst thing in the world, especially as she had no idea when she'd next have some more. Mr. Nowak hadn't told her when he paid the wages, and Sam rarely told her anything, aside from what she was doing wrong, of course.

Luckily for Eddie, Martha had thought of everything, and she arrived home an hour later to a stocked fridge and a note instructing her to help herself for as long as she needed to.

A crunchy green apple called her name. She took it, and her precious new music, to the room she and Martha used as a practice studio and set eyes on her treasured Stradivarius for the first time in a week. In an instant, her troubles faded away and she shut the door on the outside world.

The Stradivarius fit under her chin like it had been made for her, like a fifth limb, and with her sheet music set out in front of her, she closed her eyes and began to play, only opening them when she came to a part in the movement that she didn't know as well as she wanted. The piece was tricky, with lots of *sautillé*, and she lost herself to it until she came to a section she couldn't seem to get right. Frustrated, she played it over and over, but her fingers and bow seemed suddenly disconnected, and she knew from past meltdowns that any attempt at force would end in tears. Hers. And lots of them.

Sighing, she admitted defeat and packed the precious instrument away, tucking it under the silk scarf she'd carried since her twelfth birthday when her grandmother—long since dead—had given it to her. The sight of it made her heart ache. The Dean family was cold and distant, too caught up in making money and flaunting it, but Grandma Dean had bucked the trend, giving most of her wealth away whenever Eddie's grandfather wasn't around to stop her. And she'd had no time for snobbery, either—a trait that Eddie found herself admiring more and more.

Out of nowhere, Eddie giggled, imagining Sam's reaction if she put that particular notion to him. *"Hey, guess what? I'm not a snob or a spoiled little rich girl. My grandmother's friend, the Duchess of Bedford, says so."*

The idea was so laughable Eddie could hardly contain herself, though the fact that she hadn't nailed her practice session worried her more than she cared to admit. The final university orchestra line-up for the summer proms was due to be announced in a matter of weeks, and she just wasn't ready, dammit.

I have to make the first section, even if it kills me. And it likely would, given the added pressure of working, *and* taking time out to apply for the financial help she'd need to complete her degree—something she needed to get started as soon as possible.

But it could all wait for now. More than anything, Eddie craved a shower and a good night's sleep—a sleep that came as easy as breathing when her head hit her pillow.

SIX

A week later, after days and days of early shifts, lectures, and orchestra practice, Eddie found herself looking forward to her first late shift at the café. So much so, in fact, that she showed up an hour early.

Sam wasn't there. Instead, she found old Mr. Nowak nursing a huge pot of what looked like cabbage, but smelled like heaven. "What on earth is that?" she blurted before she registered the odd wave of disappointment that Sam's absence fuelled.

"Chlopski posilek. Polish peasant food. You can have some later when it's done."

Eddie peered into the pot, absorbing the fact that the Nowak family was indeed Polish. "Are those the sausages you serve for breakfast?"

"That's kielbasa, missy. Better than the rubbish you English people eat."

"I don't eat any kind of sausage. I'm a vegetarian."

Mr. Nowak's eyes narrowed suspiciously. "A what?"

"I don't eat meat."

"Why not?"

"Because I don't like it."

"You eat potatoes?"

"Yes."

"Mushrooms?"

"Yes."

"Good, then you can eat the kluski śląskie. Put some flesh on your bones."

Mr. Nowak muttered something else in Polish and returned to his pots and pans. Eddie left him to it and fetched her apron from the staffroom. When she returned, she realised that she didn't actually have a clue what to do. With no breakfast service to set up for, she was at a loss, and regretted not bothering to ask what the café served the people of Vauxhall on Friday nights. *Kluski śląskie, maybe?*

"Don't just stand there, missy. Light the candles. My grandson says you're a good worker. Don't prove him wrong."

Eddie blinked. "Sam says I'm a good worker?"

Mr. Nowak grunted, engrossed in his melting pot of sausage and cabbage. "Of course he does. You wouldn't work here if he didn't."

Good to know, but Eddie still couldn't quite believe it. She wandered around the empty café, lighting tea lights and the larger candles that were dotted around. The flickering glow was pretty and soothing and gave the café an ambiance it lacked in daylight, and Eddie found herself smiling, though she dreaded the onslaught of business that was bound to come when rush hour started.

But. *Sam thinks I'm a good worker.* Despite the irritation that bloomed whenever she thought of him, that he'd complimented her to his grandfather made her grin so hard her cheeks ached.

And she was still smiling when the man himself appeared an hour later. He greeted her with a curt nod and immediately began arguing with his grandfather in Polish. Eddie couldn't make head nor tail of their heated exchange and tried to make herself scarce.

"Where do you think you're going?" Mr. Nowak roared. "Come back here and tell this boy to stop bossing me around."

Eddie froze in her attempt to sneak past Sam and his grand- father. "Erm—"

"Leave her out of it," Sam growled. "She doesn't give a shit about either of us."

"Hey!" Eddie spun around to face Sam's fierce scowl. "That's not fair."

"True, though, isn't it?" Sam challenged. "Pops is flipping his lid because I want him to go home and put his feet up. I'm pissed off because he's calling me a lazy git for my trouble. Who's right?"

"If your point is that I don't care," Eddie said. "Then who's right is irrelevant."

"Whatever." Sam turned back to his grandfather and continued the conversation in Polish.

Eddie took her cue to turn tail and slink back into the café. In her absence, a few customers had filtered in, mainly older men who had the same accent as Mr. Nowak. They pointed to the red wine on the shelves behind the counter and sat themselves, leaving Eddie at a loss. There were no menus anywhere, and the only food to be seen was Mr. Novak's big pots and pans, the names of which had completely escaped Eddie.

She searched her brain for the last time she'd eaten in a restaurant that wasn't the French food Ian insisted on every time they went out. *Water. I'll get them some water.* She rummaged under the counter and turned up a couple of carafes. A lemon caught her eye. She sliced it up and added it to the water-filled carafes and carried them to the two occupied tables.

"Do you know what you'd like to eat?"

The men at the tables glanced up, and most of them smiled, though their responses made even less sense to her than the argument still going on by the door.

"I'm sorry," she said. "I'm new here and I don't speak Polish."

The man nearest her reached out and patted her arm. "We eat whatever Artur and Samuel have cooked tonight. Do not worry about us."

Fair enough. Eddie left the old men alone and returned to the counter. By then, more elderly men had appeared. She served them red wine and lemon-spiked water, and peered into the bubbling pots, wondering just how long Sam and Mr. Nowak were planning on tearing lumps out of each other. The old men seemed relaxed and at ease, but the breakfast shifts she'd worked had taught her that hungry customers didn't stay that way for long. What on earth was she going to do when they started demanding their dinner?

"You gonna stand there staring all night, or what?"

Eddie jumped and spun around to find Sam right behind her, his glare a weary incarnation of the one he wore most mornings. "I'm not staring, I'm paying attention."

"To what? The cabbage?"

"Piss off," said Eddie crossly. "I'm just wondering what your grandfather is planning on serving tonight."

"Nothing. I sent him home." "You *sent* him?"

Sam had the grace to share a soft, sheepish smile that

changed every facet of his entrancing face. "Well…pushed, if we're splitting hairs, but not before he told me to feed you a bowl of his kluski śląskie, which means he likes you, though I don't know why. It's not like he's seen you do any actual work."

Lacking an intelligent retort, Eddie poked her tongue out and returned her attention to the pan of cabbage and sausage. "I know what this one is. Is it the only main course you have on?"

"Yes. We serve the barszcz first, which is a soup, then the kluski śląskie and the chlopski posilek. And that's about it, apart from wine and a few gallons of coffee. They won't want anything else."

The way Sam's gravelly voice wrapped around the Polish words did odd things to Eddie. Her blistering hangover from the previous week was long gone, but her head swam as she gazed at him, lost in the molten magic of his brown eyes. She leaned closer, drawn to him. For a brief moment it seemed that he was drawn to her too, but then he blinked, and the haze around them evaporated like it had never been there at all.

Sam reached for a large metal bowl. "Ready to earn your keep?"

"Um…I guess?" Eddie watched him drain a pan of boiled potatoes and add them to the bowl, and then tip in flour and seasoning. "What are we making?"

"Your dinner, apparently. Don't mind getting your hands dirty, do you?"

"Of course not."

"Sure about that? You don't seem the type."

"Stop telling me what type of person I am," Eddie snapped. "Just tell me what I need to do."

Unfazed, as ever, by any sharp word Eddie threw his way, Sam proceeded to instruct her in the art of mixing and shaping small potato dumplings that looked a lot like the Italian gnocchi that Eddie had eaten before.

Sam rolled her eyes when she said as much. "There's nothing Italian about them. Look, stick your thumb in them like this. See? Nothing like gnocchi."

Eddie had to admit that he was right. In particular, the dumplings she'd shaped looked more like doughnuts. "What now?"

"We cook them, obviously." Sam dropped the dumplings into the largest pan on the stove and simmered them briefly in salted water until they floated to the surface. Then he disappeared into the kitchen and returned with a pan of mushroom sauce.

Eddie's mouth watered as Sam tossed the sauce and dumplings together, reminding her that she'd eaten nothing but fruit, eggs, and cheese for days. "That looks amazing."

"It ain't bad." Sam added pepper. "But you won't get any until we're done, so stop your drooling and help me plate up the soup."

Eddie did as she was told, distantly surprised at how much easier following Sam's direction was when he wasn't acting like a prize git. She thought about telling him, but serving the collection of elderly Polish men kept her too busy for the next hour or so, and by the time she'd cleared the main course plates from the tables, she didn't have the energy.

She took her final tray into the kitchen and loaded plates into the dishwasher. "Coffee now, right?"

"Right," Sam said. "Then we'll have our own dinner."

Eddie couldn't wait. The Polish food had looked so delicious that even the meat dishes had made her stomach rumble. She served twenty-three mugs of coffee in record time, and then rejoined Sam at the counter.

He passed her a heaping plate of kluski śląskie that he'd topped with paprika and a drizzle of sour cream. "Sit. Eat."

Eddie didn't need telling twice. She sat at the nearest table and dug into one of the nicest plates of food she'd ever had. It took her a while to notice that Sam had joined her, and was picking at his own food, apparently more interested in the short work she was making of hers. "I can't help it," she said with her mouth full. "It's so good."

"So I see."

Eddie swallowed. "What's the matter? You don't like women who eat, or something?"

"I like women just fine, thanks."

Eddie didn't doubt it. Sam Nowak was probably a lothario… a womaniser, and the thought of him surrounded by crowds of beautiful girls was almost enough to put her off her supper.

Almost, because she wasn't giving up her plate until she'd licked it clean.

A change of subject was definitely in order, though. "So, how much do you charge for everything we served tonight?"

"Charge?"

"Yes…charge. You don't give it away for free, do you?"

Sam took a sip of the red wine he'd brought to the table. "Erm, maybe?"

"What?" Eddie frowned, which usually earned her the sharp end of Sam's tongue, so she reached for her own tumbler of wine and took a healthy swallow. "Okay, you need to enlighten me, unless there's a punchline I'm missing."

"Punchline? To what? I'm not joking and you certainly ain't laughing."

"That's because your jokes normally leave a lot to be desired," Eddie retorted, though it didn't escape her notice that this was the first time Sam had ever looked her in the eye and uttered her name. *God, why does it matter?*

But it did.

It mattered a lot.

Hot under the collar, Eddie drank more wine. Sam did the same and pushed his half empty plate Eddie's way, silently inviting her to finish up the kluski śląskie he'd left. "Can't waste it if we're giving it away, eh?"

The mushroom-smothered dumplings were too tempting to ignore. Eddie dragged the plate towards her and dug in, much to Sam's apparent amusement.

"Where do you put it all?"

"Hollow legs," Eddie said. "Anyway, enough about my glut- tony. Explain to me how you can afford to give away twenty- three meals every night? Because it is every night isn't? The man with the trilby told me he's here every day."

Sam shrugged and tucked a pendant Eddie had never noticed into his T-shirt. "Pops has always done it since he came over here in the sixties. Times were hard then, but our peasant food is cheap to make, so it didn't make sense to watch people go hungry."

"That was sixty years ago."

"So? Not everyone has the means to become something different. Besides, those men over there...they're our friends now, our family. We have the time and the food to give, and so we give it."

Though admirable, it struck Eddie as slightly absurd. Jimmy's did a roaring breakfast trade, but surely that didn't cover opening the café every night for free. Or did it? Truthfully, she had no idea, and so she kept her ignorance to herself. "What happens now?"

"Nothing." Sam leaned back and flicked a switch on the wall. Low music filled the café. "This lot will sit around until midnight with the Dire Straits and coffee while I clean up, then I'll lock the doors and go to bed."

"You sleep here? Where?"

Sam treated Eddie to another mirthful grin. "In the kitchen…on the counter, obviously. We're poor immigrants, remember?"

"Nonsense, you were born in Leeds. Stop pulling my leg."

"Why? You make it so easy."

"You're such a buffoon." Eddie finished her second plate and shoved it away. "Where do you really sleep? Is there a flat above here?"

"Yeah, though half of it's full of my grandmother's things."

"Does she live there too?"

"No. She's in a home in Pimlico. That's why I'm here…to help Pops so he can go and see her every day."

"Oh." Eddie didn't know what to say, and the revelation cast a new light on the enigmatic young man who had hardly left her thoughts since she'd met him. "How long have you been in London?"

"Seven years."

Eddie absorbed that and studied Sam's face. When he wasn't scowling, his features were boyish and young, but also timeless, and it was clear he was the kind of man who was going to age like a dream.

Sam allowed her scrutiny for a moment, drinking his wine, then he sighed. "What are you staring at now?"

"You," Eddie admitted. "I'm trying to work out how old you are."

"Older than you."

"I know that, but it's not by much, is it?" "Depends how old you are."

Arsehole. Why does he always have to make things so difficult?

"I'm twenty-two," Eddie said. "And I think you're about a year older than me."

Sam snorted. "You think I'm twenty-three? Man, I take it all back. You can stay."

Eddie didn't know whether to be offended or intrigued, but her insane curiosity won out. "All right, all right. No need to laugh at me. How old are you?"

"Twenty-six."

Oh. "Well, I wasn't that far out."

"Far enough for me to let you go home. Go on. I'll finish up here."

"What?"

"Go home," Sam repeated. "There's not much left to do."

Even if that had been true, there was no part of Eddie that had any desire to leave the café—to leave *Sam*—just yet. She stood and picked up their dirty plates. "Thanks, but I'd rather pull my weight."

Sam didn't argue, and with two of them hitting the kitchen with what seemed like an odd compulsion to outwork the other, the clearing up was done in no time at all.

"Seriously," Sam said for the third time. "You can go. I'll be fine."

"I don't want to go." "No? Why not?"

Abruptly, Sam was standing very close to her, though he hadn't actually moved. Eddie swallowed, sure that he'd hear the stampede that her heart had struck up, that he'd feel the sudden heat in her blood. "Because—um—"

She had no words. The kitchen, steamy from the sink and

the dishwasher, closed in on her, and so did Sam. He backed her into the counter and bent his neck so their faces were inches apart. "Why do you want to be here when you have the rest of the world at your feet?"

"I don't have anything at my feet."

"Liar."

"Am not. I don't work here for fun."

"No?" Sam dragged his tongue slowly over his bottom lip.

"What if I told you I'd pay you until the end of the night. Would you go home then?"

"No."

"Why not?"

Eddie sucked in a breath and stretched up to meet Sam as he grew ever closer. His kiss was a hairsbreadth away. Her pulse raced so fast that her entire body throbbed, but just as their lips brushed, the bell on the counter rang.

Sam pulled back without looking at Eddie and strode out of the kitchen. She gazed at his retreating back, her heart in her mouth, her blood rushing in her ears, and her mind a whirling dervish of frustrated confusion. How had this happened? How had she gone from hating Sam Nowak to mourning the loss of a kiss she'd never dreamed of until now?

And what on earth was she going to do when he came back to the kitchen?

Eddie had no idea, and it turned out not to matter, because Sam never returned to the kitchen. He spent the next hour bidding good-bye to the old men as they filtered out and dumping the last of the dirty mugs on the counter for Eddie to collect and take to the dishwasher.

It was close to midnight when he handed her a broom. "Sweep. I'll mop, then I'll walk you home."

"You don't need to do that."

"*You* sleep on the kitchen counter then, 'cause you're not wandering around out there on your own."

His tone left no room for argument, and as Eddie swept, she couldn't help musing that his grouchy chivalry was a marked change from Ian who rarely gave a damn how she found her way to and from his Greenwich flat. Did Sam's concern for her well-being mean anything? Or was her relationship with Ian simply a bigger waste of time than she suspected?

Either way, Eddie finished her wine and watched—with a fascination that couldn't be healthy—Sam mop the café floor. His lean biceps and strong forearms, his elegant hands as he gripped the mop. She couldn't see his face, but in her mind she saw his concentrated frown, his bottom lip caught between his teeth the way it was when he manned the grill. She couldn't deny that he was still an arsehole, but there was something about him—*everything* about him—that set her on fire.

"You ready?"

Eddie blinked. Sam was in front of her, his apron gone, revealing a heavy metal T-shirt that, in contrast with her cashmere V-neck and high-waisted tube skirt, made him seem even more dangerous than usual. "Um, I s'pose so?"

"You don't sound so sure. What's up? Forgot where you live?"

"Very funny." Eddie took off her own apron and retreated to the staffroom to fetch her bag. When she returned, Sam was at the door, apparently in a hurry to get going.

Eddie joined him and they left, together, walking side by side so close that to a distant observer, they might've been holding hands.

Except they weren't holding hands, and Eddie didn't even

want to, because her insatiable draw to him wasn't like that. She wanted more than that.

Less than that.

More.

She didn't even know.

They reached her garden flat. "This is me."

"Nice," Sam said. "I pictured you in one of those yuppie blocks by the shops."

"How else have you pictured me?"

Sam bit his lip. "Eddie, you don't want to know."

SEVEN

Inviting Sam in for coffee was almost laughable, though the glint in his eye as he stepped over the threshold was anything but funny. He glanced around, then settled his dark gaze on Eddie. "Flatmate?"

"Yes, but she stays with her girlfriends at weekends." "Girlfriends, eh? Do *you* have a girlfriend?"

"No."

"Shame."

"Is it?"

Sam shrugged. "Maybe not."

Eddie's breath caught in her chest. She backed into the flat's small kitchen space, biting her lip as Sam tracked her every step until they mirrored their position from the café kitchen—her back against the counter, caged in his arms, enthralled by the heat of his lean, hard body.

And God, what heat. Eddie felt it everywhere—every facet and nerve. And she craved more…much more. "Sam—"

"What?" he demanded, though his tone wasn't unkind. "You want to pick up where we left off?"

"Yes. Kiss me. Sam. Please."

For a heart-stopping moment, she feared he would refuse. That she'd blink and his heated snarl would morph into the sneer that she knew so well. But the sneer never came, and instead her world was blown apart by his crushing and consuming kiss.

He crashed his lips onto hers, kissing her with his whole body, pushing her back into the counter, the rough denim of his jeans scraping her skin. She gasped, and Sam lifted her off her feet and up on to the kitchen counter, forcing his way between her legs.

"*Oh!*" Eddie arched her back, pressing her body against him, and her legs widened so she could wrap them around his waist, drawing him in, as his lips moved to her neck, sucking.

Sam bit down on Eddie's tender flesh. She moaned and shoved her hands into his dark hair. "I want—I want—"

"What?" he whispered. "What do you want from me?"

Eddie didn't know, she could only feel—feel his rough hands roaming her body, his teeth at her throat, and the hardness in his jeans pressing where she needed it most.

She had never been so turned on, so wet. Every part of her tingled—her skin, her nipples, and between her legs. Her breasts, craving the heat of Sam's touch, begged to be free.

Desperate, she pulled back slightly and yanked her jumper over her head. Beneath, she wore black lace that shaped and lifted her breasts. Sam smirked and then buried his face between them, pulling the fabric back with his teeth, until he found her left nipple. He took it in his mouth, flicking it with his tongue. Eddie cried out and threw her head back. "Oh God...yes."

More wet warmth pooled between her legs and she tightened her grip on Sam, frantic with a need for friction that even in her dirtiest fantasies she'd never imagined.

Perhaps sensing that she was fast approaching a precipice they couldn't come back from, Sam paused in his beautiful assault on her breasts. "Do you want this? Do you want me?"

"I—God, I want…please don't stop."

"Stop what, Eddie? What do you want?"

Want. The repetition of the word fought through the haze of lust and desire, and for a fleeting moment, Eddie considered the question, and only one answer was forthcoming. She opened her legs wider and took Sam's hand, guiding him under her skirt and to her silk knickers. "I want you…and I want to come. Now. Please, Sam…please make me come."

She'd never spoken so brazenly. Never wanted to. But the need to feel Sam inside her was overwhelming. And Sam heard her plea. He pushed her knickers aside and found his mark as though he'd touched her this way a thousand times over. His probing fingers slipped inside her, and his thumb brushed the bundle of nerves that made her blood sing. She cried out again, her body convulsing with jolts of pleasure, and a whisper of fear ghosted through her mind. *He's doing this with his fingers and I can hardly stand it.* The thought of what he could do with his cock—

No. Eddie couldn't contemplate it as she writhed at Sam's mercy, the sensation of slowly…wonderfully, falling apart already too much to bear.

But then, as she wavered on the cusp of a crashing orgasm, Sam withdrew his fingers and straightened up. Stunned, Eddie stared at him, her jaw slack, her eyes unblinking. *Don't stop. Please don't stop.*

The fear was real and strong, and panic threatened the

over– heated bubble she'd cocooned herself in with Sam's devilish touch. "Sam—"

"Are you on the pill?"

"Yes."

"Where's your bedroom?"

Eddie inclined her head to the left, and in a heartbeat found herself whisked off the kitchen counter and down the hall.

Sam kicked her bedroom door open and deposited her on the bed, dropping to his knees and then covering her with his body. His rough kiss returned. Eddie arched up into it, seeking friction, and skin—*Sam's* skin. *I need to touch him.*

She clawed feverishly at his clothes, his T-shirt first, and then the heavy buckle on his belt as he unclipped her bra and tossed it over his shoulder. Her breasts were finally free, and they dropped, heavy and full, into Sam's waiting hands. He squeezed them gently, and brushed his thumbs over her nipples in much the same way he had her clit in the kitchen.

And with his cock digging into her groin, the effect was only magnified. Eddie gasped shakily and bit down on her bottom lip to contain a louder exclamation. Her hands roamed Sam's broad back, and she lost herself in his smooth inked skin in an effort to retain an ounce of composure.

But she failed, spectacularly, as Sam set to work stripping her of her remaining clothes. Her skirt disappeared, and then her underwear, and then his fingers were suddenly back where they'd been in the kitchen—probing, searching, and teasing shudders and sounds from her that seemed to belong to someone else.

She raised her hips and rode his fingers, chasing the breaking sensation she'd had a taste of before—

Sam pulled his fingers back—again. Eddie growled in frustration. "Don't *stop*. I swear to God—"

"I'm not stopping." Sam rose up on his knees and finished what Eddie had started with his jeans. "You wanna come, don't you?"

"Yes."

"Good, cos I'm going to fuck you, Eddie, and you're gonna come on my dick."

He stood and shoved his jeans down his legs, kicking them away as his rigid cock sprang free. Eddie's mouth watered. She'd only blown Ian a couple of times, and had never been sober enough to truly remember it.

And she'd never been so desperate to taste him as she was to taste Sam.

She sat up and crawled on her knees to where Sam stood. His dick was so tantalisingly close to her mouth, but he shook his head. "Nah. Not tonight. You wanted to come, remember? Now turn around."

Eddie shivered, but every bone in her body was compelled to obey. She turned on her knees, and the heat of Sam's palm hit her back a second later, pushing her forwards so her chest hit the bed.

And then his cock brushed the wetness between her legs, and she cried out as shocks of pleasure rattled through her. *Oh God, he's going to fuck me.*

The fear returned, but it was tempered by a primal desire she'd never felt before. Ian and a few teenage disasters had been the only men she'd ever slept with, and the vague enjoyment she'd found with them had barely scratched the surface.

And Sam wasn't scratching, he was demanding—dominating—sure and strong as he eased inside her, gently at first, but then harder, *much* harder, as he pulled out and slammed back in again. "I'm going to fuck you. Only your word will get me to stop."

She wasn't going to ask him to stop. God, no. His cock felt so right inside her, rigid and throbbing—*pulsing*. It fit like a glove, and every stroke of it brought her to life as Sam gripped her hips and pounded into her, hard and rough, but with a rhythm that was almost graceful—melodic.

A coil of pressure built in Eddie's belly, winding tight. She cried out with every thrust of Sam's dick inside, every dig, every scrape. And his bruising grip on her hips sent the waves of heat off the stratosphere. *Oh God, oh God, I can't handle this.*

Her legs collapsed. Sam fell with her and crawled onto the bed, covering her body with his own. The weight of him was briefly comforting, but then he started to fuck her again, brutally digging his cock in and out of her. She gasped and a jolt of plea- sure hit her. Sweat trickled down her face, her back, and melded her and Sam together as he thrust inside her.

Blinded by the inferno building deep in her belly, Eddie clawed desperately at the sheets, fisting and twisting. And then Sam groaned, a ragged, primal sound that pushed her over the edge, and every nerve in her body exploded. *"Oh!"*

Her vision darkened and her mouth fell open, fixed in a silent scream. The pleasure was blinding, consuming, and her body spasmed and juddered like she'd been shocked from the inside out. Because she had, and as Sam stiffened and groaned again behind her, and an extra jolt of heat pulsed where they were joined, Eddie flew...flew so high she was sure she'd never come down.

But she did come down, whimpering as aftershocks spread through her and Sam continued to fuck her with sharp, jolting thrusts. "Oh fuck."

Sam chuckled, though it came out as more of a grunt as he finally stopped screwing her. "That what you wanted?"

"Yes." Eddie's words were muffled by the bed covers mashed into her face, but with Sam still inside her, nothing on earth could've made her move. She pushed back on him, absorbing the last flutters of the first real orgasm she'd ever had. "God, yes."

"Me too." Sam's lips were at her ear. "You're annoying, but I wanted to fuck you from the moment I saw you."

It was so close to the exact sentiment running though Eddie's hazy mind that she couldn't be offended, and so she said nothing, only whimpered as Sam withdrew from her and shifted onto his back.

Eddie rolled over too and stared at the ceiling, her body still a live wire of jittering heat. She glanced over at Sam. It was late, and as he lay there with his eyes closed, more peaceful than she'd ever seen him, she wondered if she should ask him to stay—and what it would be like to wake up to him the following morning. Would she look into his eyes and see regret, or some- thing more? Or worse, *nothing*…just a realisation that she'd just been a quick and willing fuck?

She had no idea, and her questions remained unanswered, because at some point, she drifted to sleep, and when she woke some time before dawn, she was alone. She opened her eyes to a cold, empty bed, with only the rumpled sheets to show Sam had been there at all.

Eddie woke for a second time around nine. She sat up with a jump, wondering what had disturbed her, and then the intercom buzzed, and her heart leapt. *Sam?* Perhaps he'd dashed out for breakfast, or coffee, or—

Does it matter?

Of course it bloody didn't. Naked, Eddie sprang out of bed and grabbed the first item of clothing she saw, a long, slouchy jumper dress that thankfully looked great without a bra. She yanked it over her head and dashed to the front door, wrenching it open. "Where did you get to—"

Her words died on her lips. It wasn't Sam, it was Ian, and his smooth, suave face was the last on earth that she wanted to see. "What are you doing here?"

Ian's blinding smile didn't waver. "I came to see you. We're off to the races today and I thought you could tag along."

"Tag along?"

"Yes. Come with us. You like horses, don't you?"

"Not really." Eddie folded her arms across her chest, suddenly aware of her protruding nipples. "And I've got lectures this afternoon, and rehearsals tonight."

"So? You can miss one day, can't you? Term's nearly over after all."

Eddie gritted her teeth. "I need to attend all rehearsals if I've got any chance of getting a spot in the first section. You know this. And I can't afford to miss lectures if I'm going to apply for a hardship loan."

"A what?" For the first time, Ian's cocksure smile wavered. "What on earth do you need a loan for?"

"My dad's bankrupt, remember? He's not paying my way anymore."

"Oh." Ian tapped his foot. "So you can't come to the races then?"

"No, I can't!" Eddie snapped, and then, as Ian blinked, clearly taken aback by her raised voice, made a decision that she should've realised months ago. "Look, you'd better come in. I think there's some things we need to talk about."

"Talk about? Like what?"

"Like us, Ian. Just come inside, okay?"

Ian relented and stepped inside Eddie's flat. She led him to the living room and parked him on the sofa while she made coffee with Martha's fancy machine. In the kitchen, it was hard not to picture herself pressed up against the cabinets, her head thrown back and Sam's fingers curling inside her. She shivered and bit her lip, heat flooding her cheeks. Sam's absence felt like a punch to the chest, but the lingering sensation of him fucking her—*owning* her—was undeniable.

The beeping coffee machine brought her back to the present. *Oh God, Ian. Why did he have to turn up today?* But all the will in the world wouldn't get rid of him, and the clarity of the decision she'd made at the front door struck her again. *I have to do this.*

And she *wanted* to do it. Resolved, she carried two bone china mugs of latte into the living room and set them on the coffee table. "I don't think we should see each other anymore."

Ian blinked. "What?"

"Us—" Eddie gestured between them. "It's not working. I think we should end things."

"End things." Ian shook his head slightly, as if to convince himself he'd heard right. "You're dumping me?"

"Not really. We were never official. And it's not like you haven't been seeing anyone else, is it?"

Ian flushed guiltily, but Eddie took no satisfaction in being right. After all, she was the one with Sam Nowak's sweat still cooling on her sheets.

"Why now," Ian asked, like he'd read her mind. "Have you met someone?"

"Not exactly," Eddie hedged. "It's just my life has changed a lot, and it's going to keep changing. We don't fit together— I'm not part of your world."

"You've never tried to be. You hate my friends, and you belittle everything I do."

It was Eddie's turn to blink. "Excuse me?"

"You can't deny it," Ian said. "I've never worked out why you've stuck around so long. You don't even seem to enjoy making love to me anymore."

Making love. Jesus Christ. Eddie refrained from scoffing.

"Ian, we weren't making love, because we never loved each other. It was just fucking, and we weren't very good at it."

"Fucking?" Ian's eyes widened. "Eddie, don't be so coarse. There's no need for language like that."

"And there's no need for you to scold me like I'm a naughty child. I'm twenty-two, Ian. I'm not a silly teenager."

"I never said you were." Ian's tone turned sulky. "I just don't get it. We look good together, everyone says so."

Eddie fought the urge to compare Ian's painstakingly gym-sculpted body with Sam's natural, lean muscles. She failed, and heat swept through her again, but she fought that too. "Ian, looking good together isn't enough. We have to *feel* something too, and I'm sorry, but I just...don't."

Ian reached for his coffee, and Eddie braced herself for a further round of negotiating, but it never came. Ian sipped his latte, and then shrugged, his frown fading to the oblivious half grin he usually wore. "Fair enough. How about the races, though? I can spot you some cash if you want to have a flutter? Maybe you'll win enough to avoid that pesky loan?"

Eddie groaned. The offer was sweet, but based on a reality

that was no longer hers. She'd yet to be paid for her work at the café, but she couldn't deny that it felt good to know whatever money she had in the bank from this point on had been earned with her own blood, sweat, and tears. "Ian, it's over. I'd like us to be friends, but I don't think we should see each other for a while."

Ian shrugged. "Oh well, can't blame a bloke for trying. I'll miss making love to you, though, Eddie. It really was amazing, wasn't it?"

It was easier to nod and smile, and drift off as Ian's wittering washed over her, his voice—that she'd once found melodic and sweet—dulling to a low drone as her mind filled with images of Sam's naked body. His coiled arms. The hard planes of his inked chest...and his cock, jutting out from his slim hips, rigid and proud. She imagined taking it in her mouth, swirling her tongue around it, sucking. Warmth pooled between her legs and she crossed them, abruptly aware of her lack of underwear.

"Are you all right?" Ian asked suddenly. "You've gone all red."

Eddie fanned herself. "Have I? Actually, Ian, I don't feel too great today. Would you mind if we caught up another time?"

"Erm...okay." Ian stood awkwardly, and Eddie realised that it was the first time she'd ever turned him away.

Fleetingly, she felt bad, but then she remembered all the mind-numbingly boring dates she'd endured, the nights she'd stayed at his place, the bad jokes, bad sex, and the *terrible* wine. *It wasn't all his fault, though, was it? He never forced you to stay.*

Of course he hadn't, but that didn't mean that she had to stay now. Or, rather, that Ian did.

Eddie hustled him to the door, hoping for a quick goodbye

— and one with no touching. Unfortunately, Ian had other idea, clumsily taking her into his arms and planting his sloppiest kiss to date on her Sam-bruised lips.

Cringing, Eddie let him have his moment, and then pushed him away. "That's enough, Ian. I'll see you around, okay?"

Ian sighed. "Okay, Eddie. Take care, won't you? And don't be a stranger?"

"I won't," Eddie promised, though she had no intention of seeing Ian anytime soon, if ever again.

She shut the door on him and let out a long breath. The next few days were her busiest yet, packed with rehearsals, lectures, and working at the café, but for the first time since she'd left Italy last year, she felt free.

EIGHT

Eddie didn't hear from Sam all day. She attended Saturday lectures and a gruelling four-hour orchestra rehearsal, and checked her phone every moment she could, but it remained blank, and by the time she left campus, a righteous anger had begun to tickle her veins. After all, Sam had fucked her and then left her without so much as a word. *How dare he?*

But her belligerence was quickly overcome by embarrassment. What was it he'd said? *"You're annoying, but I fucked you anyway?"*

Not quite, but paraphrasing suited her mood.

She went home, half-hoping to find Sam on the doorstep. Of course, she didn't, and she considered passing by the café, but pride kept her at home. Instead, she washed Ian's coffee cup, took a shower, and climbed into a bed that still smelled of Sam Nowak.

The next day was the first Sunday that Eddie had been asked to work. She turned up to her breakfast shift all guns blazing, but found old Mr. Nowak cleaning the grill.

"Sam doesn't work most Sundays," Mr. Nowak growled

out. "He looks after his *babcia* for me and cooks the dinner at my house. You'll see him tomorrow."

Bastard, though Eddie knew she couldn't slate Sam for taking care of his grandparents, when it had been the one thing that she'd immediately liked about him.

Irritated, she got to work filling the condiment bottles and the salt and pepper pots. When that was done, Mr. Nowak called her to the grill. "You want to cook today?"

"Cook?" Horror shuddered through Eddie. "Me?"

"Why not?" Mr. Nowak countered. "My grandson is always complaining about being tied to the grill. Let him clean the tables."

Despite herself, Eddie grinned, and didn't point out that Sam cleaned plenty of tables when she was around. She took Mr. Nowak's spatula and studied the flat top of the grill nervously. "How do you scramble eggs on this?"

"I'll show you. Don't worry. Sunday is a different crowd to the rest of the week. They shout less."

Eddie wasn't sure she believed him, but she followed his instructions on setting up to cook anyway. Sam and his grandfather ran the grill, the toaster, and the hot plates single-handed, often making hot drinks and serving on the till at the same time. Eddie, apparently, would spend the morning limited to just the grill—bacon, sausages, mushrooms, and eggs. Black pudding and the café's famous bubble and squeak. Tomatoes and fried bread. The idea of handling the deeply-scented kielbasa sausages made Eddie feel slightly ill, but the challenge of cooking for Vauxhall's hungry breakfast crowd was oddly exciting. And really, how hard could it be to flip a few bits of meat and fry some eggs?

Very, as it turned out, and even though Eddie had far fewer

tickets in front of her than Sam or Mr. Nowak ever had, she struggled to keep up.

"You got that bubble, missy?" Mr. Nowak roared. "Customers waiting."

"It's coming," Eddie snapped. Then she scanned the grill and realised the *delicious* dollop of crushed potatoes and vegetables she'd slopped on the grill was perilously close to catching fire.

Damn it. She scraped it into the bin, hoping Mr. Nowak wouldn't notice that it was the third portion she'd ruined. Or the collection of overcooked eggs she'd stashed under an empty bacon packet.

The morning rushed by in a haze of singed mushrooms and sausage grease. Eddie was taken aback when Mr. Nowak pried the spatula out of her hand and told her it was time for her own breakfast. "Already?"

"It's midday. Let's eat."

Eddie wasn't about to argue. At Mr. Nowak's instruction, she fixed herself a plate of eggs, mushrooms, and bubble and squeak, and him a collection of as much meat as possible, topped off with a huge pile of grilled tomatoes.

At the same table Eddie and Sam had sat at on Friday night, Mr. Nowak cast a critical eye over her plate. "Still no meat?"

"I'm a vegetarian," Eddie insisted for the millionth time. "Besides, not starving myself, am I?"

Mr. Nowak couldn't argue with her heaping plate and dug into his own breakfast. Eddie did the same, and for a while they ate in companionable silence, washing their food down with big mugs of Mr. Nowak's special sweet tea.

The taste of it took her back to the morning she'd rocked up on his doorstep, and she wondered what he made of her now. Apparently Sam thought her a good worker, but what about Mr. Nowak? Did he think she was worth the tea, toast, and shelter he'd bestowed on her that fateful wet morning?

Mr. Nowak's face was as unreadable as Sam's when he wasn't roaring for plates of burned bubble and squeak, and it was on the tip of her tongue to ask, but that's not what came out when she opened her mouth. "Did you see Sam yesterday?"

Oops. But Mr. Nowak didn't seem bemused by the question. "'Course I saw him. He brought me the takings last night and got a clip round the ear for his trouble."

Eddie couldn't help smiling. "Really? Why was that?"

"Because he's rude. All morning he has a face like a smacked behind, and then he's still sulking when I see him later. That boy needs to cheer up."

Eddie's smile faltered. "He was in a bad mood?"

"He's always in a bad mood."

A few days ago, Eddie would've been inclined to agree, but with the image of him bearing down on her, his lips curled in a wicked smirk, so fresh and raw, she couldn't deny that she'd seen another side of Sam—a side she was already darkly addicted to.

I want to fuck him again.

The realisation shocked her, and delivered another dose of the devilish heat she'd carried since Sam had first laid a hand on her. Mr. Nowak said something. She blinked. "Sorry. What?"

"You kids." Mr Nowak shook his head. "You're all the same—away with the fairies. At least you eat, though, and take care of yourself. Not like that grandson of mine."

Eddie frowned. "What do you mean?"

But Mr. Nowak's answer was cut off by the arrival of a

group of people he clearly knew. Eddie forgotten, he rose and rushed to greet them, leaving her to clear the table and get back to work. Which she did until Mr. Nowak sent her home.

It was gone three when she let herself into an empty flat. Her cryptic conversation with Mr. Nowak still on her mind, she took a shower, and then went to the spare room and spent the rest of the day mastering the passage of music she'd been unable to get right all term.

Vanquishing that particular demon was liberating, but she couldn't dissuade her Sam-obsessed brain from returning to Mr. Nowak's assessment of Sam's mood the previous day. His absence from Eddie's bed now made sense—he'd gone to open the café, of *course* he had—but his subsequent black mood stung. Had she been that bad in bed?

Eddie's self-esteem was precarious enough to wonder, but her memories of that night wouldn't have it. The connection between her and Sam had been dangerous—explosive—and undeniable. It wasn't that. It couldn't be.

Perhaps it's got nothing to do with you. Ever think of that?

Eddie thought about it now, and decided it was a convenient truth that she could live with. Sam's radio silence bothered her more than she cared to admit, but there was no doubt in her mind that Sam fucking her like that, so hard and raw, had been as good for him as it had for her.

Right?

She was no closer to figuring it out when she arrived for her early shift on Tuesday morning and found Sam already there, hacking up tomatoes and mushrooms like they'd run over his dog.

"Morning," she said hesitantly. "Um…I've brought my violin with me because I have uni after work. Is there somewhere safe I can store it?"

It wasn't quite the breezy, nonchalant entrance she'd planned, but being in Sam's presence again had tripped her up, wiping her brain of coherent thought. It even took her a few moments to notice that Sam's answering chuckle held little humour.

"Figures," he muttered darkly.

"What does?"

Sam tossed his knife on the counter and showed her his face for the first time since he'd left her splayed out on her bed. "That you're one of those posh music students who walk around town with their noses in the air. Let me guess. Daddy bought you such a prized instrument that the insurance policy is more than your rent? And you want me to hide it upstairs for you so the poor people don't see it?"

His tone was so scathing that Eddie took an instinctive step back, though he wasn't wrong. Her Stradivarius *was* worth more than the car she'd left at her parents' Buckinghamshire estate, and the monthly insurance bill she'd recently become responsible for made her eyes bleed.

Eddie met the stern glare Sam was treating her to. "Is some– thing wrong?"

"Nope."

"Sure about that? You seem to be in a bad mood."

"I'm just fine, thanks. Are you working, or what? Don't pay you to stand around the kitchen."

"I'm going to get changed now, I just need—"

"Yeah, yeah, your crown jewels. Give it here, I'll take it upstairs."

Nonplussed into silence, Eddie handed over the violin,

cringing as Sam took it and stormed out of the kitchen, letting the door to the café bang noisily behind him.

"Pissed him off already?"

Eddie jumped a mile and whirled around. At the back door stood a man around Sam's age who clearly shared his taste in sinfully tight jeans and Motörhead T-shirts. "Who on earth are you?"

"Dylan," the man said easily. "I came to see Sam, but I guess I'll leave if he's in that mood."

"That mood?"

Dylan grinned, flashing Eddie a set of perfect white teeth. "Yeah, *that* mood. The one where he growls a lot and punches walls."

Brilliant. As charming as Dylan seemed to be, Eddie couldn't raise a smile. What she'd expected from Sam, she wasn't quite sure, but the proverbial kick in the teeth had fallen way short of the mark. "I'm going to get changed."

Dylan nodded, and Eddie left him to his doorway leaning, assuming he'd have found something better to do by the time she came back.

He hadn't, and Sam was still absent too, and so nothing had changed. Eddie got to work rescuing the produce that Sam appeared set on pulverising, and when Dylan ventured further into the kitchen and perched himself on the counter beside her, she cast him a curious glance. "You must be pretty good friends with Sam if he lets you sit on the counter."

Dylan reached across Eddie and snagged a tomato. "He's my best mate, not that I ever see him. He's always holed up here, or running around for his grandparents."

"That's what I'm here for," Eddie said absently. "To give him and his grandfather more time to themselves."

"Well, you're not doing a very good job. I haven't seen Sam

for a week, and now I come by to find him in one of his rages."

"Excuse me?" Eddie began indignantly, then she looked up again and caught the mirth in Dylan's gaze. "I'm not responsible for Sam's moods. That man is a mystery to me."

The last part was true, but Eddie couldn't shake the worrying inkling that she'd inadvertently riled Sam's temper. Though quite how, she had no idea, aside from the now dismissed theory that she was simply a crap shag.

On cue, Sam appeared in the kitchen. "Your violin is on my couch. Better hope my cat don't piss on it."

"You don't have a cat," Dylan piped up before Eddie could have a coronary.

"How would you know? You haven't been round for weeks."

"One week, actually," Dylan countered. "I came by last weekend, but your grandpa said you were having trouble—"

"Shut the fuck up."

The vehemence in Sam's growl turned Eddie around, but he wasn't looking her way; he was glaring daggers at Dylan, who appeared unrepentant, though he said no more.

Eddie went back to her chopping. Dylan flashed her a cheeky wink that set off his blue eyes and hair that was as light as Sam's was dark, then he slid sinuously off the counter and followed Sam out of the kitchen.

Nice to meet you.

Eddie shook her head slightly as she tipped her prepped produce into the large plastic containers Sam and Mr. Nowak kept in the fridge beneath the grill. In his own way, Dylan was as intriguing as Sam, and the exchange of two men who were apparently best friends had left her a little bemused. *Shut the fuck up.* Why? What had Dylan been about to say that Sam didn't want her to hear?

And why did she care when he so clearly didn't give a stuff about her?

The righteous anger that had niggled at Eddie since Sam had initiated radio silence returned full force. *I've had enough of this.* She rinsed her hands under the tap and then stalked out of the kitchen in search of Sam. Dylan be damned, she was having this out with him right now.

But Sam was nowhere to be seen, Dylan either, and Eddie's frustration boiled over. She slapped her hand down on the nearest table, absorbing the impact as it rattled up her bow arm and into her shoulder blade, prodding an old injury she couldn't afford to awaken. Damn Sam Nowak. *I hate him.*

The abrupt onslaught of emotion, along with the sound of footsteps on the stairs, sent Eddie running back into the kitchen. She was back at her chopping station when Dylan reappeared.

"Yup. He's in a stinker, all right," he said.

"Not my business." Eddie looked in the fridge for bubble and squeak ingredients. "I'm sure he'll get over it, though."

"Doubt it, but do me a favour, will you?"

"What's that?"

"Make sure he eats something before you get busy. He doesn't look after himself."

Eddie frowned. That was the second time she'd heard that in as many days, and coming from Dylan who didn't look much older than her, it sunk in all the more. *He doesn't look after himself.* What did that even mean?

Clueless as ever—when it came to Sam Nowak, at least—Eddie didn't know, and when Sam came back to the kitchen, his scowl firmly in place, she decided that she didn't care.

He'd survived twenty-six years without her concern. *Let him stew.*

But her resolve grumbled instantly a little while later when she came out of the kitchen, weighed down by a tray of full milk jugs, to find Sam slumped at a table, his head on his arms.

Eddie set the tray down and moved quickly to Sam's side. She touched his arm and immediately felt the heat radiating through his T-shirt. "Sam? What's the matter?"

Sam's response was muffled by his arms, but the set of his shoulders gave off his message loud and clear: *Leave me alone.*

Fine.

Eddie went back to the counter and noisily stowed the jugs away by the fruit juices. She half-expected Sam to yell at her for chipping crockery, but when that didn't happen, she glanced at him again to see that he hadn't moved.

Eddie checked her watch—five minutes to six—which meant the café was about to open. Dylan's request flashed into her mind. *"Make sure he eats something before you get busy."* Though Eddie couldn't think why Dylan had felt the need to drop by at the crack of dawn to say such a thing, his instruction was something she could actually do.

Flicking the toaster on with one hand, she rummaged for bread with the other. She retrieved four slices of the cheap white bread the café's patrons preferred and chucked them under the heat.

She searched for something to put on it. Butter, obviously, and then a jar of honey caught her eye—London honey, from a hive down the road.

When the toast was as dark as it could go without burning, Eddie rescued it and slathered on the honey. She took two slices on a plate, and a glass of orange juice, to Sam and banged them on the table.

Clearly startled, he raised his head, his face pale and drawn. "What's that?"

"Breakfast," Eddie snapped, fighting the urge to brush his wayward hair out of his face. "Eat it and pull yourself together. I can't serve everyone by myself."

She forced herself to walk away and get on with the last few jobs setting the café up without checking back on Sam. A few minutes later she felt, rather than heard, him get up and go into the kitchen. She had no intention of following him, but as the clock struck six and the front door keys were nowhere to be seen, she sighed heavily and barged through the kitchen door.

Sam was by the freezer, jabbing something that looked suspiciously like a needle into his abdomen. He jumped when he noticed Eddie, and thrust whatever it was into his pocket.

Oh no you don't. Eddie strode to him and shoved her hand into his pocket. "What on earth are you doing? Are you bloody mad?"

Perhaps taken by surprise, Sam didn't react, and Eddie had her fingers around something small and plastic before he suddenly moved and ripped her hand out of his pocket.

The plastic object went flying across the kitchen and clattered into the sink. Eddie wrenched her hand free of Sam's vice-like grip and lunged for it, snatching it and holding it up in the air. "What the hell are you doing? Does your grandfather know about this?"

"About my insulin pen? Yeah, I'd say so."

"Your what?"

"My insulin pen." Sam crossed the room in two strides and

pried Eddie's fingers open. "What did you think it was? A fucking smack fix?"

Eddie opened her mouth. Shut it again, as she realised that she actually had no idea what she'd been thinking when she'd thrown herself at Sam. Just that her imagination had driven her to assume the worst. That the sight of him injecting God-knew-what into his stomach had terrified her. "I'm sorry."

"Whatever." Sam turned away.

Eddie grabbed his arm. "What do you need it for? Are you diabetic?"

"What do you think?"

Sam glared at her like she was London's biggest idiot, and for once she agreed with him. Dylan and Mr. Nowak's cryptic comments now made sense, and so did the state she'd found Sam in. As she watched him shovel back the toast she'd made him, it was obvious that the plate of toast and honey was doing him the world of good. The dull haze faded fast from his usually sharp eyes, and colour returned to his his chiselled cheeks.

Eddie longed to touch him, to feel the warmth of his blood rushing beneath his smooth skin, *and* check his temperature had gone down, but something—*everything*—in Sam's stance kept her still. "I'm sorry," she said. *Again.*

In answer, Sam dropped his empty plate on the counter and walked away.

And the silence remained in place for the rest of the day. Sam ignored Eddie's attempts to break it, and only spoke when he needed her to do something. The lack of communication wasn't that unusual, but with the scent of Sam still clinging to her skin—in her imagination, at least—Eddie took it to heart, and around mid-morning, she realised that the band of painful tension in her head was because she was fighting tears.

Eddie never cried, not even when her beloved grandmother had died of a stroke on Christmas Eve. No. She was a fighter, a scrapper, and she'd be damned if she let Sam Nowak dictate every moment of everything that passed between them.

Resolved, she took a deep, shaky breath, and marched into the kitchen. Sam was at the fridge, retrieving packs of bacon to restock the counter. "Look," she began. "I'm sorry I jumped on you over something that's none of my business, but it's really not fair of you to treat me this way, especially after—"

"After what?" Sam cut in fiercely. "You think I owe you a conversation? Just because I fucked you the other night?"

The brutal candour was so close to Eddie's worst fears that she took an instinctive step back. "Just because you *fucked* me? Is that all it was? An empty hook up?"

"You tell me."

"I'm asking you."

"Why?"

Eddie shook her head in an attempt to clear it. "Why— what? I don't understand."

"Like hell, you don't." Sam shut the fridge with a bang. "It ain't hard, is it? You fancied a bit of rough, and I gave it to you. Now you can go back to your fancy-pants world, and I can stay here in mine, jacking up smack in the kitchen, 'cause that's what you thought, isn't it?"

Eddie couldn't deny it, and her silence was an open door for Sam to rip her apart.

He sneered and shook his head. "Yeah, you thought I was scum that first time you laid eyes on me, and nothing's changed, has it? I can make you come, but I don't wear enough tweed for anything else."

Sam laughed humourlessly and made to brush past Eddie, but she caught his arm, digging her nails into his forearm. "That's not fair. I don't care if you're my boss when your grandfather isn't here, you don't get to talk to me like this."

"No? Why not? Too up your own arse to hear the truth?"

"*What* truth?" Eddie shouted, what was left of her composure evaporating in a cloud of Sam Nowak-themed dust. "I haven't got a clue what your problem is. You're the one who left me in bed like some cheap tart you'd picked up down the pub."

Sam raised an eyebrow and looked pointedly over Eddie's shoulder. She followed his smirk and saw that she'd neglected to close the kitchen door behind her and the whole front row of the café was now looking their way with considerable interest.

Furious, her face hot with humiliation, Eddie released Sam's arm and slammed the door. "Are you going to tell me what your problem is, or am I just to assume that you're a complete bastard?"

"Assume whatever you want," Sam countered. "Won't get you nowhere."

Eddie shook her head. "Trust me, there's nowhere I'm going but home. I've had enough of this crap for one day."

"See you then."

"That's it?"

Sam shrugged. "Got everything else you wanted, didn't you?"

"*I* did? You—" Eddie stopped, whatever words she'd had stuck in her throat, because what else was there to say? Sam had played his hand and his position was clear: Eddie had been nothing more than a cheap shag—a crap one, if the cool mocking in his usually molten eyes was anything to go by—

and he couldn't care less if she screamed blue murder in his face, or left without another word.

And so she left, grabbing her coat and bag and storming out of the café with her apron still tied around her waist. She was on the bus to orchestra rehearsals by the time she remembered she'd left something vital behind.

I hate him.

Cursing the day she'd laid eyes on Sam Nowak, and his wonderful gruff and kind grandfather, Eddie jumped off the bus at the next step and ran the half mile back to the café.

Sam was at the counter. He glanced up as she barged through the door and pointed to the ceiling. "Key's under the box of napkins. Your shit is on my couch."

Eddie stalked past him to the door that led upstairs, and on the second floor of the building, found a landing crowded with boxes of café paraphernalia. She found the one labelled "napkins" and retrieved the key to the locked door on the other side of the hall.

It felt odd to let herself into Sam's flat while they were on such bad terms, but despite her hurry to grab the Stradivarius and get to rehearsals, Eddie couldn't contain her curiosity as she glanced around the neat and tidy space that Sam called home. There wasn't much to it—just a living room with a sofa- bed, a tiny kitchen, and a closed door that she assumed was the bathroom, but it smelled amazing—it smelled of *Sam*.

Eddie started to smile, but then her gaze fell on a small bag of medical supplies on the table and choking tears once again caught in her chest. *It's not all his fault, remember? You messed up too.*

She couldn't deny it, nor the guilt as it burned in her chest. She grabbed the Stradivarius with shaking hands and fled the flat.

It was her intention to slip out of the back door, but Sam was in the small yard outside, heaving a bag of rubbish into the giant red bin.

Eddie steeled herself and approached him, silencing her phone as Martha's ringtone—"The Nutcracker"—blared from her pocket. "Look, I'm sorry about today, all right? I didn't know you were diabetic, and you're right—I made assumptions about you that I should've have. Perhaps that makes me all the things you say I am, but that doesn't mean I deserve the way you spoke to me."

And this time she walked away with her head held high.

NINE

Eddie slid her bow into its protective sleeve and packed it away in her case. Rehearsals had gone well—*really* well—and despite her dreadful morning, she was flying.

Martha appeared at her side and nudged. "Oh my God, you smashed that solo. If you don't get a first chair now, there's something seriously wrong with the world."

Eddie could think of plenty of things that were wrong in her world, but in this she had to agree with Martha. She *had* smashed it, and the nod from the orchestra director had solidified her joy as the rehearsal had come to an end. Still, counting her chickens was terrifying, given her current situation. "Do you really think I'll get a chair?"

"Of course," Martha said. "You're the best of the seconds, and there's two places up for grabs. If you don't, I'll start a protest."

Eddie giggled. "You're such a goob. Thanks, girlie."

"Don't thank me yet. I'm about to drag you home to finish your loan applications."

Eddie groaned. "Really? But I'm so tired. I worked all morning."

"You'll be even more tired if you have to quit uni and work in that hell hole full time."

"It's not a hell hole," Eddie protested, though the café had felt like one this morning, and the thought of spending the rest of her natural life there was enough to make her shudder. "How long will the applications take?"

"No idea," Martha said cheerfully. "But I've started them for you. We just have to fill in the technical bits I didn't know."

"I love you. You know that, right?"

"Yup. Now let's go. I don't want to be up all night."

Not wanting to be up all night turned out to be wishful thinking on Martha's part, as it was well past midnight by the time Eddie's collection of loan and grant applications were complete and submitted.

Martha sloped off to bed, muttering something about a life- time supply of Yankee Candles when Eddie hit the big time, while Eddie shut down her laptop and took a much needed shower, hoping it would soothe her wired brain enough for her to sleep.

And as ever, when her thoughts were unguarded, as the hot spray eased her tired body, her mind turned to Sam. Her parting words to him had been more than justified, but she couldn't hide from the guilt that burned a path from her gut to her soul. Sam had a lifelong condition, a disease that likely affected him each and every day, and she'd practically called him a no-good junkie.

What the hell is wrong with me? Eddie turned her face to the water, like it could cleanse her brain of the privileged life and mindset she'd enjoyed until a few weeks ago. Was she really that judgemental and shallow? Because if she was, then she deserved most of the anger Sam had thrown her way.

Most, because there was no way that the deep yearning she felt for him was a simple crush on a man who represented everything her life had been missing. No. Her attraction to Sam was real, even if it was highly likely that they'd never again share a civil word—a fact that despite her own regrets was *definitely* not all her fault. And it wasn't like this was the first time that Sam had been a complete dick. Sighing, she turned off the shower, wrapped herself in a towel, and padded to her bedroom. The flat was dark and quiet, but the urge to lock herself in the spare room and toil away on her violin was strong—so strong that she actually dressed in loose pyjama bottoms and a camisole, before she remembered that it was one o'clock in the morning and Martha was sleeping.

Damn it. Eddie threw herself on her bed and stared at the ceiling. This was the kind of night when she usually wound up calling Ian and heading out into the night for a glass of dreadful wine and some bad sex, but she'd shut that door now, and she had no regrets.

Just a tingle between her legs and brain that wouldn't quit reminding her of the one time she'd been sexually satisfied.

Sexually satisfied? Eddie giggled out loud. That was one way of describing the earth-shattering orgasm Sam had brought her to, and the memory of it went some way to easing the hurt that her encounter with him today had left behind. Unbidden, her hand drifted to her waistband—

Something clattered against her bedroom window. Eddie jumped a mile. *Shit. What was that?* Likely a bird, or the wind, but Eddie's heart struck up a tattoo anyway, her hand frozen guiltily in place, her body tense.

Thunk. Thunk. Thunk.

In a flash, Eddie was up. She wrapped the blanket from her bed around her shoulders and dashed to the front door, ignoring her father's warnings about wandering the city in the middle of the night.

She ran out into the street, and there was Sam, sitting on the pavement by her bedroom window, flicking tiny stones at the glass. "What are you doing here?"

"I brought your wages," Sam said flatly. "I was going to post them through the letterbox, but I figured I'd find out if your toff boyfriend was man enough to come out here and see what all the noise was."

"My *what*?"

Sam laughed in the humourless way Eddie hated so much. "Your blond hunk of Harrods. What's he doing? Sleeping off his Dom Perignon buzz?"

"...*blond hunk of Harrods*..." Eddie searched her brain. "Oh God, are you talking about *Ian*?"

"That his name, is it?" Sam stood and held out a small brown envelope. "Figured it would be Cuthbert, or some shit."

"Stop it," Eddie snapped. "Ian's not my boyfriend, and he never was. Besides, I'm not seeing him anymore, not that it's any of your business."

"Dumped you, did he? Was that before or after you had him in your bed a few hours after me?"

The pieces of Eddie's Sam-shaped puzzle suddenly clicked into place. She pictured the moment Ian had left her flat the morning after she'd slept with Sam, and it all made sense. "Did you come back here the morning after, um—"

"The morning after I fucked you? Yeah, I did, but I didn't get very far. Your boyfriend was already here."

"He's not my boyfriend."

"Sure looked like it."

"I'm sure you looked like my boyfriend too, to anyone who looked through my window that night."

"Fucked him too, did you?"

"No."

"But you have."

It wasn't a question, but Eddie nodded anyway. "Yes, on and off for nearly a year, but I *told* you. I'm not seeing him anymore. That's what I was doing that morning, breaking things off."

"Why?"

It was hard to tell if Sam cared about Eddie's answer. She stepped closer to him in the darkness and took the envelope from his outstretched hand. "Because I wanted to. Things were never right between him and me—the company, the sex, it was all bad, and I'd finally had enough. If that makes me some kind of slut in your eyes, fine."

Eddie started to turn away. Sam grabbed her arm, his fingers closing around her wrist in a bruising grip. "Why then? Why now? If you've been seeing him all this time?"

Eddie shrugged. "What do you want me to say? That...*fucking* you showed me the light? That I hadn't had a real man until you made me come?"

"If that's the truth, yes."

Eddie gazed up at Sam, lost instantly in his eyes now the harsh edge that made her heart shudder had eased a touch. "You made me feel like I deserved better, that I deserved to *feel*, even if you never touched me again, so yes, *Sam*. You showed me the light. Now, are you going to let me go, or are you coming in?"

Leading Sam to her bedroom was nothing like it had been the first time around. The heat was still there, but the urgency had faded to a dull roar.

Eddie sat on the edge of her bed as Sam leaned against the closed door. "Do you want something to drink? To eat?"

Sam shook his head. "I'm good."

Eddie nodded and leaned back. It was a subconscious invitation, and Sam took it, crossing the small room with two silent strides and covering her with his body, pressing his forehead to hers.

"I don't like you."

Eddie smiled. "I don't like you either."

"So why am I here?"

"You tell me."

In answer, Sam kissed her, his lips a mind-bending contradiction of hard and sweet, his hands rough, and yet conversely gentle.

Eddie melted into his embrace, arching her back, and hitching her leg over his hip, clawing at his chest, tugging at his hair, desperate for whatever he had to give.

Sam slid his heated palms over her belly and up beneath her camisole, cupping her breasts—kneading, squeezing, brushing her nipples to hardness with his calloused thumbs.

Eddie shivered, her body instantly and wonderful alive in a way she'd only ever felt with Sam. She broke their kiss and sank her teeth into his neck, drowning in his scent, bewitched by his answering groan as he bore down on her.

Sam released Eddie's breasts and pulled her camisole over her head. His eyes darkened, and he licked his lips. "Been dreaming about your tits."

He said with a smile that softened words that might other- wise have felt crass to Eddie's sheltered ears. She brought her own hands to her breasts and squeezed them, pinching her nipples and arching her back. It was perhaps the moment to tell Sam that she'd been dreaming of his cock, but she didn't.

Instead, with her gaze still locked on him, she hooked her thumbs in the waistband of her pyjama bottoms and pulled them down. Sam's eyes widened as he apparently absorbed her brazenness, and then they flashed with an emotion Eddie couldn't decipher as he ripped her pyjama bottoms down her legs and tossed them aside.

He grabbed her ankles and yanked her to the edge of the bed. "You wanna come again?"

At his mercy, Eddie nodded. "Yes."

Sam grinned, and then dropped to his knees, burying his face between Eddie's legs.

"*Oh!*" Eddie cried out, rearing up from the bed as Sam's tongue found her clit and swirled around it, sending heat roaring through her before she had time to comprehend what he was doing. *Oh God, oh God, he's going down on me.*

No one had ever gone down on Eddie, not even Ian—*especially* not Ian—and now she knew why she'd never bothered to ask, because there was no way another man could make her feel the way Sam was now. His lips, his tongue, the oh-so-light scrape of his teeth. She sobbed with the intensity of it, only her fist in her mouth muffling her screams.

She came quickly, convulsing as orgasm rushed through her, her legs wrapping in a vice around Sam's head, pinning him in place as wave after wave crashed over her until she was finally spent.

But Sam was apparently far from done with her. He broke the stranglehold Eddie's legs had on his neck and stood, quickly shedding his clothes, leaving only the metal pendant that was now so obviously a medical ID that Eddie wanted to cry.

His cock distracted her, as magnificent as she remembered, long and thick and hard, and the desperate craving to take him in her mouth returned full force, but Sam was too quick for her. He grabbed her ankles again and pinned her legs above her head, plunging inside her before she'd caught her breath.

For a moment he held wonderfully still, giving her time to adjust to his size, and then he began to move, slowly at first, teasing her with each thrust, until she dug her nails into his chest and silently demanded *more*.

Sam picked up the pace and fucked her as brutally as he'd done the first time, slamming into her, pounding, driving all coherent thought from her. A rag doll beneath him, she gasped and her eyes rolled, her cries once again muffled by her hand in her mouth.

Climax hit her hard and fast, and Sam came quickly too, stiffening as Eddie fell to pieces, the sharp drive of his cock faltering to become erratic. He released her legs, dropped his chest to hers, and groaned into her neck, thrusting into her a final time before he went utterly still, his dick pulsing heat where they were joined.

Eddie fell slack, her hands buried loosely in Sam's hair as she counted his laboured breaths, the beat of his heart hammering against hers, anything to tie her down to a world that had narrowed in the last half hour to become all about Sam Nowak.

She couldn't say how long she'd been holding him when he finally raised his head, and his face was unreadable. For a fleeting moment she feared that he would pull away from her and leave again.

But he didn't leave. He kissed her cheek and scooped her into his arms, before lifting her to the head of the bed and snag- ging the rumpled covers to drape over them both.

Being in bed with Sam was a strange feeling. Eddie rolled over and propped herself up with one elbow as Sam did the same. "Are you okay?"

She half-expected him to scoff and sneer, but he fixed her with an intense stare and nodded. "I am now, and I guess I owe you an apology. Seems it ain't just you that jumps to conclusions."

"I can see why you thought what you did, though. There's no excuse for what I did, Sam, and I really am sorry."

"Don't be. It's not your fault that I was having a bad day."

A bad day. Eddie pictured Sam slumped at the café table and her heart skipped a beat. "What happened?"

Sam shrugged. "Sometimes I can do everything right, take my shots, eat all the right shit at the right time, and it still fucks with me. Having breakfast chucked in my face definitely helped, though."

His laughter eased the worry in Eddie's heart. She gave in to the urge to kiss him and drove her tongue sweetly into his mouth, before she pulled away and returned to the matter at hand. "How long have you had it?"

"Diabetes?"

"Yes."

"It runs in my family. I was born with it."

"I'm sorry."

"Why?" Sam rolled onto his back. "I don't know any

differ- ent, and I'm okay most of the time. I'd probably never have told you if you hadn't walked in on me."

Eddie wasn't sure how she felt about Sam never trusting her enough to tell her something so important. "Does Dylan know?"

"Dylan?"

"I met him this morning—yesterday morning, I think? I liked him."

Sam grinned. "I like him too."

"He said he was your best friend."

"He is."

The distinct sensation of missing something washed over Eddie, but the sensation was brief, and quickly overcome by Sam idly trailing his work-hardened fingers across her belly.

"What's your real name?" he asked suddenly.

"My real name?"

"Yeah. Don't tell me it's Eddie. Posh people aren't born with names that cool."

That he thought her name was cool was almost enough to make her jump him again. "It's Edwina, obviously."

"Lady Edwina?"

"Of course not! My dad's a stockbroker, not a bloody earl. At least, he was."

Eddie's humour faded as quickly as it had come on, and, perhaps sensing her shift in mood, Sam sat up, leaning over her, his eyes gleaming in the dim light of the room. "Is he dead?"

"No, just broke. He went bankrupt a few weeks ago."

"Bankrupt?"

"Yes, as in bust. His business folded and he's lost every-thing—job, house, cars. He's even stopped paying my tuition and rent."

"Ah." Sam nodded, like Eddie's appearance in his life suddenly made sense. "But don't you go to that fancy uni in New Cross?"

"Goldsmiths?"

"If you say so."

Eddie rolled her eyes. "Yes, I'm a student at Goldsmiths."

"So how are you going to pay for it working part time in my family's crappy café?"

"Your grandfather offered me forty hours a week, and the café isn't crappy and you know it, but to answer your question, I won't need to pay for it all myself up front. I've applied for some loans and grants to help me out. My wages from the café will top up my rent and keep me fed."

"Hey, you won't ever go hungry while you work for Pops. It's against his religion."

"And yours, as best I can tell. Apparently, the only person you don't feed is yourself."

"Very funny." Sam stuck his middle finger up, and then leaned backwards over the side of the bed in a startling show of flexibility. When he straightened up, he was holding the envelope he'd given Eddie in the street. Somehow, in their haste to fall into bed, it must've ended up on the floor. "You'll be needing this, then."

My wages. Eddie sat up and took the envelope, her hands feeling oddly shaky as butterflies flitted around her stomach. "You know, I'm so naive that I thought this would somehow find its way to my bank account, even though I never gave your grandfather my details. It never occurred to me that he'd pay me in cash."

"He's old fashioned," Sam said. "And his bank charged him a penalty fee about a decade ago. He's never trusted them since. Are you going to open it?"

"I don't know if I dare. I should probably take it straight to the bank in the morning."

"It is morning."

Eddie glanced through the crack in the curtains. The sky outside was still as black as tar. "No, it's not."

She opened the envelope anyway and fanned out the crumpled notes inside like it was the first money she'd ever held. In the grand scheme of things, it wasn't much, but to her, it was everything, and Sam seemed to know it, even though he said nothing as she gazed at the fruits of her own hard work.

"I wish I could save it all for next year, but I need to find my rent for the next few months before my loans kick in—if I get them."

"Are things really that bad?"

"Worse," Eddie said with a sigh. "This is great, but after my rent and bills, it only leaves me about twenty quid a week to live on. Good job I have the Nowak family feeding me, eh?"

Sam smiled slightly, his half grin lighting up the dark. "I'd say it's working out for all of us right now."

"Thought you didn't like me?"

"I don't, but I like fucking you."

TEN

Bright sunlight woke Eddie the next morning—sunshine that was far too bright for the dawn alarm she was sure she'd set. *Shit!* She bolted upright, her heart in her mouth, before she remembered that it was Wednesday and she wasn't working until the evening.

And then she remembered Sam too, and glanced to where he'd fallen asleep beside her, fully expecting to find empty space. But—

He stayed. And more than that, he was still fast asleep, stretched out on his back with one arm flung over his head. *God, he's gorgeous*, and though Eddie was loathe to disturb him, her hand found its way, unbidden, to his chest, her palm resting instinctively over his heart.

On cue, Sam woke, opening his eyes with a slow smile that brought his face to life in a way Eddie had never seen before. "Mornin'."

"Morning," Eddie said tentatively, still half convinced that she was dreaming. "Don't you have to work?"

"Nope. Dylan's doing it. He helps out from time to time when he's not busy with his own shit."

Eddie pictured Dylan lounging on the kitchen counter and his easy demeanour suddenly made sense. "He never said he worked at the café."

"That's because he doesn't really. Hasn't since he graduated and got a real job. He only does it once in a blue moon to give me a day off."

"That's nice of him."

"I know, that's why he's my mate."

"Your best mate."

"Yes."

Eddie couldn't say why it mattered, but it did. She'd never seen Sam and Dylan together, but the subtle burn in their eyes when they spoke of each other was exactly the same. "I like him."

"He liked you too."

"Really?"

"Yes. He said you were nowhere near as stuck up your own arse as I'd said you were."

"Charming."

Sam shrugged. "*I've* never claimed to like you."

Eddie couldn't argue with that, and knowing that she'd made a good first impression on Sam's best friend felt better than she cared to admit. Mr. Nowak liked her too, so perhaps Sam's issues with her were all his. *Or a healthy dose of sexual tension—*

"What've you gone all red for?"

Eddie blinked. Sam was all up in her face, smirking, like he'd read her mind. "I'm not all red."

"Are so."

"Bloody hell!" Eddie pushed him away. "You'd say black was white just to disagree with me."

Sam laughed and rolled away. "Only because you're always wrong."

"Am not."

"Yeah, yeah." He sat up. "Keep telling yourself that. I gotta go."

"You're leaving?" Disappointment joined the heat in her chest as Sam got out of bed.

"I didn't bring my insulin with me and I've got some errands to run for Pops."

"Thought it was your day off?"

"It is. I'm going out with Dylan later, if you want to come? Though I don't reckon you'd enjoy where we're going."

Eddie bristled. "Who are you to tell me what I enjoy?"

"Like metal clubs, do you?"

"Don't know. Never been."

Sam snorted. "There's a reason for that." "You're an arsehole."

"Yup." Sam pulled his clothes on, and Eddie mourned his lean, flawless torso as it disappeared. "But you're still welcome if you fancy slumming it more than you have already."

"Slumming it how? By working at the café, or fucking you?"

"Ouch."

Eddie sat up, clutching the bed covers to her chest. "Yeah, well. You deserve it, and unfortunately, I can't come out with you tonight. I'm working with your grandfather at the café."

"Fair enough." Sam stamped into his battered boots. "Shame, though. I'd have liked to see you in a mosh pit."

"Why?"

"Because—" Sam came back to the bed and leaned over Eddie, pushing her down. "—you, missy, ain't as clean cut as you make out. Reckon you'd be right at home, all grimy and shit."

Eddie wrinkled her nose, hoping her face didn't give away how hot Sam's words made her, because the idea of being grimy and dirty with him anywhere—even a grotty heavy metal club—made her wet between the legs.

Sam's ever-present smirk deepened, and his eyes blazed. "What are you doing today? Got somewhere to be?"

"Not until later."

"Good. Now get on your knees."

Much later, after making Eddie come twice with his talented tongue, Sam finally left, and after a quick shower, it was time for Eddie to head to uni.

Her lectures seemed more boring than usual, because despite her sometimes unhealthy obsession with her own performance, Eddie had little interest in the history of Romanticism and its legacy in popular music. She took idle notes, and doodled Sam's name in the margin. At one point, she scrawled Dylan's name too, which unnerved her enough to switch her focus to the lecturer droning on at the front of the classroom.

Shame he'd finished for the day.

Eddie gathered her things and ran for the bus, the days of when she'd stopped for a chablis and then hailed a taxi a distant memory. At the café, she instinctively looked for Sam, but he wasn't there, and neither was Dylan, and Mr. Nowak was in one of his grumpy moods.

All evening, Eddie stirred pots of Polish sausages and poured red wine, but she couldn't seem to do anything fast enough for Mr. Nowak's liking.

"Why are you still messing with that pot? People are waiting all night for their food!"

"I'm coming, I'm coming," Eddie snapped, and swept out of the kitchen with her arms full of plates...straight into Dylan. "*Oh.* It's you."

Dylan smiled. "The very same. You'd better come back to say hello, though. Artur looks like he's about to blow a gasket."

It took Eddie a moment to twig that he meant Mr. Nowak —a moment too long if Mr. Nowak's furrowed brow was anything to go by.

Squeezing past Dylan, Eddie hurried into the café and delivered the last main course plates of the evening, then she returned to the counter where Dylan was waiting. "Are you here to meet Sam?"

"Yup. He's not here yet, though. Running late, as usual."

Eddie had never noticed Sam running late, but then, the only times she'd seen him outside of the café, they'd been fucking in her bed.

Dylan apparently didn't share Sam's gift for reading Eddie's mind. Instead of Sam's devilish smirk, his smile was innocent as he poured himself a glass of Polish red wine and decamped to the "staff" table.

"Come and join me when you're on your break," he called.

A nice theory, but for once Mr. Nowak didn't seem obsessed with feeding her. Instead, he was hell bent on pulling out the freezer and cleaning behind it, a task Eddie couldn't let him attempt on his own, even if he could've fit behind it.

Which meant she spent her break on her hands and knees, and not in the good way. She was up to her eyes in grease when Dylan popped his head into the kitchen to say goodbye.

"I'm meeting Sam down the road now," he explained. "You want to come meet us later?"

"Thanks, but I'm a little too grimy, even for whatever crap-hole Sam's dragging you to."

"It's me that's doing the dragging, actually," Dylan said. "Sam's too anti-social for clubs. He only comes so he can complain about it."

Eddie scrambled inelegantly to her feet. "Even so. I don't think he'd be very pleased if I showed up like this."

Dylan grinned. "Sam gave me the impression that you don't care all that much what he thinks."

"I don't, but still." Eddie turned to the sink and turned the taps on, hoping Dylan wouldn't notice her flush. "I've got work tomorrow morning, and rehearsals after that. I need an early night."

"I'll bet."

Eddie glanced up. "Excuse me?"

"You've been working a lot," Dylan said. "This place exhausts me, even when it's quiet. I can't believe I'm going out tonight. Sam will probably have to carry me home."

Eddie felt equal parts guilty for assuming Dylan was ribbing her, and oddly warm at the thought of Sam's arms around him. *Jesus. What's wrong with me?* "Well," she said. "Have a nice time. I'm glad I got to see you again."

Dylan smiled and lightly punched her arm. "Me too—hey, take my number. Maybe we can have lunch some time when these Nowak's haven't got you chained to the sink."

They exchanged numbers and he left, and he'd been gone more than an hour when Eddie realised that she had his number, but no way of contacting the man who by now had turned her inside out more times that she could count.

How the hell did *that* happen?

ELEVEN

Later that evening, Eddie found herself wide awake and roaming her bedroom, doing her best to keep quiet as Martha slept next door. She'd told herself that she didn't want to go out, that she had no interest in *"slumming it"* at a grotty rock club, but alone in her room, at one with the accompanying silence, she craved company…stimulation. She craved *Sam*, in any way she could have him.

It was a crying shame that she had no way of telling him.

Unless…

Eddie glanced at her phone which she'd set to silent when a bunch of girls from her course had added her to a group chat about some lame end of term party. Dylan's number was on her missed calls list from where he'd called her earlier to give her his number. Her thumb hovered over it. Dare she call him and ask for Sam? What would Sam make of that?

After all, *he* hadn't given Eddie his number. Perhaps he didn't want to hear from her.

Yeah, 'cause he probably wants this all on his terms. Whatever *this* was.

Growling her frustration, Eddie tossed her phone on her bed. Even without worrying what Sam would make of it, she couldn't think of a sensible reason to call Dylan. At least, not one that didn't make her sound like some kind of maniac.

"Sorry to bother you, love. But would you mind if I interrupted your night out to borrow your mate? I'm feeling kind of horny over here."

Eddie laughed out loud, couldn't help it. Maybe that was the problem—that she was horny, even though Sam had sated her that very morning. Was that how it worked? The more sex you had, the more you wanted? Dear God. Eddie didn't think it was possible to want Sam more than she did already.

I still hate him, though. And it was mostly true. Sam's mind-blowing touch didn't take away from the fact that he was the rudest and most exasperating man she'd ever met.

Which made her agitation now all the more annoying.

And, impossible to ignore.

Eddie snatched up her phone again and opened WhatsApp. A text wasn't as desperate as calling, right? If she sent one innocuous enough, she could even claim that she'd sent it to the wrong person.

But what to say? Eddie drummed her nails on the screen, and then tapped out a message that she hoped conveyed a casual and impersonal attempt at conversation. *Having a good night? Bet you're having a wilder time than me!*

She was tempted to add a photo of her fluffy slipper socks to further add weight to her girlfriend cover story, but the thought of Sam seeing them stopped her.

Here goes nothing. She sent the message and then set her phone carefully by her pillow, and lay down. It crossed her mind to turn the phone off so she wouldn't have to spend the rest of the night staring at it, but with a curious anticipation bubbling in her veins, she couldn't bring herself to do it. Not that she was seriously expecting a reply, mind. Men didn't go in for texting, right? And Sam had already proved himself the master of silence.

But you didn't text Sam…you texted Dylan.

The pedantic devil on Eddie's shoulder had her sitting up again. What if Dylan got the message and showed it to Sam, and they both had a good laugh about it? And worse, what if Sam then told Dylan all about him and Eddie? How she'd got down on her knees and taken his cock? How she'd splayed her legs and begged him to make her come—

Eddie's phone rang, buzzing on silent into her pillow. Startled, she lunged for it and turned it over. *Dylan.* Oh God. What was she going to say? What was *he* going to say?

Stomach in her mouth, she took the call. "Hello?"

Silence, and then a dark chuckle that definitely wasn't Dylan's. "Do I need to worry about you flirting with my mates?"

Eddie bit her lip. Sam's voice did wonderful things to her, but embarrassment warred with the thrill dancing through her. "I wasn't flirting. I was just asking him if he'd had a good night."

"He did."

"Wonderful. Did you?"

"Yup."

"That's all you called to say?" Eddie could hear music at Sam's end, and shouting, and wondered if they were still at the club. "Because, really, you could've told me tomorrow."

"And you could've asked me tomorrow. But you didn't. You asked Dylan. Tonight."

"Dylan's the one who gave me his number."

"You want my number, Eddie?"

Damn it. Eddie closed her eyes. Sam Nowak would be so much easier to resist if he never said her name. "If you like. I can't promise I won't keep texting Dylan, though. He's much nicer than you."

"Most people are. I'll text you my number when I get home."

"Okay."

"G'night."

"Night."

Eddie lowered her phone as Sam ended the call, and stared at the screen. Sam hadn't sounded like he was anywhere close to home, but she was willing to bet that she'd find no sleep until he made good on his promise.

And she was right, of course. It was gone three by the time her phone finally buzzed under her pillow, the screen flashing with a message from an unknown number.

From Sam.

Goodnight, Eddie x

"Congratulations, Eddie."

Eddie beamed and shook the orchestra director's hand. "Thank you...thank you so much. I won't let you down."

She returned to her chair—her old chair—and glanced to the right to where she'd be sitting the next time the orchestra rehearsed. Chair six in the first section! Not only had she been promoted, but she'd jumped a row too. Unable to contain her glee, she searched the woodwind section for Martha and held up six fingers.

Martha pumped her fist, her message clear: *You've earned this.*

And it was true. The hours she toiled away in the café was paying her rent, but this was the reward of *years* of hard work, and the pride in her heart was so strong it hurt.

She was still on cloud nine when she danced into the café the next day for her evening shift.

Mr. Nowak shook his head. "You youngsters are like newborn lambs when you're happy, no?"

Eddie set her bag and violin on the counter. "Are you comparing me to a sheep?"

"If the shoe fits. What are you doing with that instrument of yours? Sam says it's expensive, so I don't want it lying around my café attracting the thieves."

Huh. Sam seemed to tell Mr. Nowak a lot about Eddie when she wasn't around. "I usually keep it in the flat upstairs. Is Sam home?"

Mr. Nowak shook his head. "No, he's off somewhere with Dylan, but you know where the key is, yes?"

"Certainly do."

Eddie gathered her things and slipped past Mr. Nowak and upstairs. Though Sam was out, she still found herself looking for him as she opened the door to his flat and delivered the Stradivarius to the relative safety of his couch. The flat was as tidy as ever, clinical almost, like no one really lived there at all. And maybe that was the point. Did the flat feel like home to Sam?

I bet it doesn't.

Either way, Eddie didn't linger. She dashed downstairs to the staff room with the rest of her things and put her apron on.

The usual evening crowd began arriving a little while later. By now, Eddie knew most of them by name and enjoyed the gentle banter that batted back and forth as she served them.

"You're still too skinny," Jurek said. "Tell Artur to feed you more."

"He feeds me plenty," Eddie shot back. "Don't worry about that."

And Eddie couldn't deny that working at the café had not only cut her grocery bill in half, but also given her extra curves she was learning to love. And Sam seemed to like them too. Eddie hadn't seen him outside of the café since he'd stayed over a week or so ago—between work, uni, and orchestra Eddie hadn't had a moment—but he seemed pleased to see her every shift they worked together, and in no hurry to let her go when he saw her out at the end of each working day.

Heat instantly bloomed between Eddie's legs as she recalled how they'd left things the day before. She'd worked until 10 pm, and with the regulars happy enough with their Dire Straits and coffee, he'd walked her within view of her flat and then kissed her, right there in the street, tipping her backwards, and driving his tongue into her mouth until she saw stars.

His kiss was hypnotic and addictive. Shame his personality was as obnoxious as ever, even if he was more prone to random acts of chivalry than any man she'd ever known—

"Are you working for me today? Or away with the fairies?" Eddie jumped a mile. Mr. Nowak was right behind her, clutching a cauldron of soup, his eyebrows dancing crossly. "Stop sneaking up on me."

"I wouldn't be able to if you were busy. Now get to work."

Eddie poked her tongue out at Mr. Nowak and did as she was told. Their working relationship had mellowed recently to become one where he shouted a lot, and she argued back, all the while working her tail off for him. It was much like working with Sam, just without the heavy sarcasm and blanket of sexual tension.

Later that evening, Mr. Nowak came to find her in the kitchen. "You have a visitor."

Eddie looked up from loading the dishwasher. "A what?"

"A visitor," Mr. Nowak repeated like she was a blithering idiot. "Shall I send her in?"

Her? For a horrifying moment, Eddie could only picture her mother, who she'd yet to speak to since Daddy had gone bust, but perspective returned quickly, and she was expecting Martha when she appeared in the kitchen a moment later.

"So *this* is where you work?" Martha glanced critically around the small, steamy kitchen. "I knew it was a greasy spoon, but I think my imagination was being kind."

"Hey!" Eddie was instantly defensive. "It's not so bad, and to be fair, there's nothing greasy about it. Mr Nowak is fanatical about cleaning."

"Yes, but, Eddie…is this really how you want to spend the next two years? Up to your elbows in dirty dishes?"

The prospect of working her fingers to the bone for the fore– seeable future was something Eddie had accepted far quicker than she'd ever have imagined. "It's a job," she said. "And I like it."

"Are you sure it's the job you like?"

"Excuse me?"

Martha arched a perfectly groomed eyebrow. "I saw you yesterday with the thug who works here, and I know you've had someone in your room. That's why I came down. Eddie, have you lost your mind?"

"What on earth is that supposed to mean?" Eddie shut the dishwasher with a bang. "And since when have you cared about my love life?"

"So you are seeing him?"

Eddie very much doubted that Sam would commit to anything that formal, but she couldn't quite bring herself to admit to Martha that she was fucking him. Or had fucked him. *Whatever*. "Look, if you just came down here to judge me, you should probably go. Mr Nowak is quite strict about slacking off, and we can have this ridiculous conversation at home."

"I'm not judging."

"No? Sure sounds like it."

"Eddie, I mean I'm not judging *you*. I just think there are better places that—"

Mr. Nowak stuck his head into the kitchen. "The music system isn't working. Check the fuse box."

"The what?"

But he was already gone. Eddie glanced around the kitchen, and then back at Martha. "Don't suppose you know what a fuse box looks like, do you?"

"What do you think?"

"Fair enough. I'll see you later, then, yeah?"

"Eddie—"

"What?" Eddie finally snapped. "Don't you realise what's going on here? What's changed? About my—about *me*? You might think this job is demeaning, but for the first time in my life I feel like I'm doing something that actually matters. That I'm contributing to the real world, instead of leeching off—"

"*Eddie—*"

"I'm not finished!" Eddie's shout rang out in the steamed-up kitchen, and as she stared at Martha's shocked face, realised that she was yelling at herself as much as anyone else. "Look, I'm sorry I'm being melodramatic about it, and in an ideal world, perhaps I'd have a job that was more…relevant to what I want to do with the rest of my life, but don't belittle what I'm doing right now, Martha, *please*. Because it's the only thing that makes any sense."

"Eddie, for goodness sake. I'm just trying to tell you that the fuse box is over there."

"Oh."

"Oh, indeed." Martha crossed the kitchen to open a cupboard above the counter where the vegetables were cut. "But for what it's worth, I am sorry for what I said. It was only because I worry about you."

"Well, you shouldn't. I'm fine."

"I know you are, and I'm proud of you. You just have this habit of diving head first into things and letting them carry you off before you've thought about the consequences. Look at you and Ian. If you'd stopped to think, you'd have realised what an absolute clod he is."

"Or you could've told me."

"Like you'd have listened. Ah, look. Here it is. That looks like a fuse box, doesn't it?"

Eddie had no idea. She stared at the mass of switches and buttons. *"Check the fuse box."* What did that even mean?

Like he'd heard her stupidity from out in the café, Mr. Nowak barged back in. "Did you fix it?"

"Um…no?"

"Move then. Let me look." Mr. Nowak shouldered Eddie out of the way and glared at the fuse box. "It seems to be fine. So why isn't it working?"

He was muttering to himself as much as to Eddie, but Martha, ever helpful, piped up anyway. "Can you plug it in somewhere else? At another power point?"

"No, it's…how do you say it, built in? Connected to the mains, and I'm not an electrician. Sam does these things for me."

"Oh well." Eddie dried her hands and smoothed her apron. "Looks like the customers will have to entertain themselves for the night, eh?"

Mr. Nowak shrugged. "Or you can play that violin of yours for them? Jurek was asking me only this evening when they would get to hear you play."

"Oh no." Eddie shook her head. "I couldn't possibly—"

"Why not? You must play for people all the time."

"In an orchestra, not a café full of old men."

"*Old?*" Mr Nowak raised a bushy white eyebrow. "You think we're too senile to know good music?"

"That's not what I said."

"Good. Then you'll play." He pointed to the guitar case Martha had tucked under her arm. "And your friend can play too. I'll pay you both extra."

He stomped out of the kitchen without waiting for an answer and apparently considered the matter settled. Eddie met Martha's wide eyes and cringed. "See what happens when you harass me at work? I'm so sorry. If you go now, I can sneak you out of the back door."

Martha laughed. "Where would I go? Home by myself to play to an empty room? Lord, no. I'm in if you are."

"Are you serious?"

Martha shrugged. "Why not? My chamber group plays at the jazz bar all the time. This place isn't that different."

"You said it was a greasy spoon."

"Well..." Martha poked her head out of the kitchen door, then looked back at Eddie. "Perhaps I was wrong. With the candles and bare brick walls, it's actually pretty cool out there. Chilled. And you could do with the extra money, right?"

Eddie couldn't argue with that, but she still wondered if

she'd been dropped into a parallel universe as she retrieved the Stradivarius from Sam's flat.

By the time she got back downstairs, Martha was already perched on an unoccupied table, picking a flamenco melody out on her guitar. Eddie hurried over and took the Stradivarius from its case. "This lot won't be interested in that. They've had the 'Sultans of Swing' on repeat for as long as I've worked here."

"Then we'll educate them then, won't we?"

Martha's impish grin was like no expression Eddie had ever seen on her. *Christ, is there something in the water here?*

Either way, she followed Martha's lead and together they kicked out a selection of classical pieces, orchestral and jazz, until the calls for contemporary rock became too loud to ignore.

"All right, all right." Eddie glanced at Martha. "You're up to date on your Dire Straits, right?"

Martha sniggered. "Of course. Play it every day."

Eddie rolled her eyes. "Don't take the piss, or one of us will have to sing."

"I'll sing."

"Are you serious?"

It was the second time in the space of an hour that Eddie had asked Martha that, and the second time that Martha's answering nod half convinced her that she was having the weirdest dream ever.

"Oh, come on, Eddie. Don't tell me your dad didn't play the *Brothers in Arms* album to you when you were little? I think I know every track word for word."

"Lucky you. My dad was never home, and my mum didn't do music unless it was locking me in the dining room to practice."

Martha giggled. "You're so dramatic. Just follow my lead, okay? You probably know the riffs by heart, even if you don't realise it."

Eddie wanted to scoff, but Martha's kind heart kept her quiet, and by the time they'd played their third Dire Straits track, she realised that Martha was right. Night after night of listening to the same album had sunk into her, and picking out the guitar riffs and solos on her violin was more freeing than anything she'd played in years.

An hour or so later, Eddie packed the Stradivarius away and gave it to Martha to take home. "Are you sure you'll be okay, walking by yourself?"

"Of course," Martha said. "It's barely midnight." "Yes, but—"

"We'll take her."

Two shadowy figures loomed out of the darkness. Martha shrank back against the café wall, but Eddie relaxed as Sam came into view with Dylan grinning beside him. "What are you doing here?"

"Live here, don't I?" Sam quipped, his eyes gleaming darkly.

"I was talking to Dylan," Eddie countered. "The whole world doesn't revolve around you."

Dylan chuckled. "Met your match there, mate. Who's your friend, Eddie?"

"Martha." Eddie grabbed her hand and yanked her forward. "She's my flatmate."

"Cool. Can I carry that for you?" Dylan addressed Martha

and pointed to her guitar case. "Me and Sam will see you home safe, won't we, Sam?"

Sam rolled his eyes. "If you say so."

And after several beseeching stares in Eddie's direction, Martha agreed to let them walk her home. Eddie watched as they disappeared into the night, noting fondly that Sam walked two paces behind as Dylan and Martha struck up conversation. She wondered if they'd come back. Tomorrow was her only free morning for the rest of the week, and she'd been kind of counting on persuading Sam to walk *her* home... and spend the night.

Bite me, Martha. Though, with any luck, Martha would've warmed to Sam by the time he and Dylan got her home.

Yeah right.

Eddie shook her head ruefully and went back inside to help Mr. Nowak clear up.

He greeted her with a frown. "Still here?"

"Where else would I be?"

"I thought you'd gone home with your friend."

"My shift isn't over."

Mr. Nowak smiled. "It is as far as I'm concerned. You played wonderfully tonight. I am very proud of you."

Eddie was suddenly and ridiculously choked. Martha aside, it had been a long time since she'd heard those words. She turned away from Mr. Nowak under the pretence of washing her hands for the millionth time. "Oh well. I'm here, so I might as well help you finish up."

Mr. Nowak said no more, though he did move around the café with more speed than his elderly body should've allowed, beating Eddie to every job. Stubborn, just like his grandson.

Eddie was about to throw in the towel and go home when

Sam and Dylan finally reappeared a little while later. "Get lost, did you?"

Sam's dark scowl was a stunning contrast with Dylan's sunny smile.

"Martha invited us in for a drink," Dylan said. "Sam's sulking because he wanted to come back for you."

"That so?" Eddie cut her gaze to Sam. "Miss me?"

"Nope. Just didn't fancy lounging around your place without you riding—"

"Sam!" Eddie thumped his arm, while Dylan laughed, though she wasn't as mortified as she might've been a few months ago. Life had hardened her in recent weeks. She raised an eyebrow in Dylan's direction. "As it goes, I don't ride him. Why have a dog and bark yourself?"

In an instant, Eddie was lifted off her feet, and her back slammed against café wall. She gasped, glad Mr. Nowak had gone upstairs to fetch more candles for tomorrow. "*Sam—*"

But he cut her off with a brutal kiss, and, Dylan forgotten, she lost herself in him, breathing in his fresh scent, tasting beer on his tongue.

He pulled away with a blazing stare that silenced any lingering retort she may have had. "Don't get lippy, woman."

Despite the heat in his eyes, there was humour too as he released her. Eddie straightened her clothes and looked over his shoulder at Dylan, who was watching them with an inscrutable expression that she was more used to seeing on Sam. "Anyway," she said, in an effort to regain her composure. "It's probably time I went home."

"Or you could stay for a drink," Dylan said.

"A drink?"

"Why not? We've had a few...we'll probably have a few more. Why don't you join us?"

Eddie should've gone home, but one glance at Sam was enough for her to know that she wasn't going anywhere, not tonight. She wanted Sam, in every way possible, and as he gathered a few bottles of red from behind the counter, having Dylan along for the—*ha*—ride was more alluring than she cared to admit.

⁂

"So…do you have a girlfriend or not?" Eddie threw back the last of the wine Sam had passed her the moment they'd come upstairs—served in a small, patterned tumbler that had been refilled more times than she could count.

Not that she was complaining. Polish red wine *rocked*, and the sensation of Sam beneath her as she lounged on his lap rocked even more.

But Sam apparently didn't speak much when he was drunk, which left Eddie and Dylan to have a conversation that so far resembled an X-rated game of Truth. "Tell me," Eddie needled. "Do you have a girlfriend? Or do you like the boys better?"

Dylan rolled his eyes and tipped the last of his own wine down his throat. "I told you already. I swing both ways, so I like it *all*. I don't have favourites."

Eddie poured more wine. Dylan had revealed his fluid sexuality quite early in the conversation, but it had taken a while to sink in, and she couldn't deny that she was utterly fascinated. Full glass in hand, she leaned back on Sam, absorbing the bite of his rough jeans against her skin. Between the wine and the talk of Dylan's sex life, a slow fire had begun to simmer in her veins. *Damn it. As if I wasn't horny enough.*

On cue, Sam's lips found her neck, nuzzling, biting, dragging his stubbled jaw along her delicate skin. Eddie tipped her head back to allow him better access. She sensed Dylan's eyes on them, and knowing that he was watching made Sam's every touch impossibly hotter.

An image flashed into her mind. Her eyes flew open and she sat up, sloshing wine over Sam's leg. "Have you two ever...er... you know? Hooked up?"

Beneath her, Sam laughed, and stood as abruptly as Eddie had sat up, lifting her away from him, and depositing her on the sofa-bed. "I need some food."

He left the flat, presumably to raid the café kitchen. Eddie watched him go, then turned her attention back to Dylan. "Something I said?"

"Doubt it. Sam doesn't care what anyone thinks, not even you."

"Not even me?"

"He likes you. Can't you tell?"

"Most of the time, not much. He's an enigma, but I like that when he's not being a total dick about it."

Dylan chuckled and reached for his glass. "That sounds like Sam, but in answer to your original question, I'd have to say...no, if what you're really asking is if me and Sam have ever fucked. Because we haven't, and we wouldn't, 'cause Sam isn't into me enough to do that."

"Isn't into you *enough*?" A jolt of heat shot through Eddie. "So he *is* into you a little bit?"

"Shouldn't you be asking him that?"

"I'm asking you."

Dylan put his glass down and considered her. "Why, though? I mean, you seem like a cool chick, but most girls wouldn't like talking about everyone their man had messed about with in the past."

"I'm not most girls. And I'm not asking about everyone, I'm asking about you."

"Fair enough. There really isn't much to tell, though, to be honest. We've slept in the same bed a few times—mainly drunk, or when Sam's been sick, and we've been…close, but nothing's happened. He isn't into blokes like that."

Close. There was another beat to Dylan's explanation, Eddie could almost taste it. She licked her lips and leaned forward. "Have you ever shared a girl?"

Dylan's eyes flashed, and he leaned forward too. "Ah, so that's what you really want to know? If we've ever taken a girl and shown her the best of both of us?"

"Yes." Eddie couldn't deny it, and with Dylan's face mere inches away, she didn't want to. Sam had entirely and irrevocably claimed her, even if he didn't know it, but there was some- thing about Dylan too. Something that she was finding harder and harder to resist.

The front door slammed shut. Eddie's heart leapt into her mouth, but she didn't move. Couldn't, because even as Sam's shadow darkened the doorway to the living room, and her body called to him, she wanted Dylan too. Just a little bit.

Just a taste.

"Pinching her already, Dyl?" Sam's tone was mild, but Eddie didn't dare look at him as he ventured further into the room, even as she absorbed Dylan's relaxed grin. "Thought you weren't game for that shit anymore?"

Dylan smirked. "Been a while, eh?"

"That it has." Sam reclaimed his space behind Eddie and wound his arms around her waist, pulling her between his legs, pressing his body against her.

The hardness in his groin dug into her back, and a thrill shuddered through her. Sam's body reacted, and he circled his hips, bringing his mouth back to its favourite place on her neck, his breath warm on her ear. "I don't know what Dylan's been telling you, but if it's something you want, you just gotta say. And if it's not, that's cool too. We're all friends here, nothing—"

"I want it." The words were out before Eddie could stop them, tumbling from her in a breathless plea. "I want both of you—and I want to watch you, together."

"Together, eh?" Sam's voice deepened. "We haven't got much in that repertoire, but Dylan likes to watch too. Maybe you can figure something out between you."

"Yeah?" Eddie's fingers were already fumbling with the buttons on her shirt. "And what will you do while we're doing that?"

"I'll put my dick in your mouth."

The air shifted. Eddie wriggled from Sam's grip and turned in his arms, throwing herself at him, claiming his mouth as her own—lips, tongue, teeth, she wanted it all.

Sam grunted, and behind Eddie, Dylan chuckled darkly. "Looks like we've got our hands full."

But Eddie didn't care about their hands. Both men could do whatever they pleased with her—all she wanted was Sam's cock in her mouth, to suck him, taste him. To undo him the way he'd undone her so many times.

Sam broke their kiss and stood, taking Eddie with him, while Dylan pulled out the sofa-bed. And then Sam and Eddie crawled onto it, stripping their clothes, as they rolled over and over, fighting for dominance in a battle Eddie was happy for Sam to win.

And win, he did. He pinned her arms behind her back and

pushed her chest into the mattress, her wet heat exposed to the night air. "What do you want, Eddie? You want to blow me while Dylan fucks you?"

Oh God. "Yes. Please. Let him fuck me."

"Sure? 'Cause you know you can stop this anytime, don't you? Dylan's a good boy. A word from you, and he'll back the fuck off."

Eddie squirmed until Sam released her and then walked on her knees to him, pushing him against the back of the sofa-bed, nudging his legs apart to make a cradle for her naked body, her gaze already locked on his thick, hard cock. "I want this. I want *you.*"

Sam said nothing more. He leaned back, his eyebrows raised in an invitation Eddie didn't need. She dropped her head and took him in her mouth, swallowing him down in all the ways she'd dreamed of while she'd waited for this moment.

His groans and gasps were as hot as she'd imagined. Hotter. And the sensation of him scraping the back of her throat sent shivers down her spine. She moaned around him, and the answering buck of his hips set her on fire.

Behind her, Dylan made his play. She heard the rustle of his clothes as he shed them, and felt the heat of his naked skin as he moved closer.

She braced herself for the head of a cock that wasn't Sam's pushing inside her. But instead came Dylan's long, elegant fingers, probing gently inside her, curling and twisting, searching for the sweet spot that Sam had found so fast.

It took Dylan a little longer, but when he did, *oh God.* Eddie pulled away from Sam to cry out, and Sam moved like a snake, shifting down the mattress to shove his tongue into her mouth.

He kissed her like a man possessed as Dylan worked his fingers inside her, bringing her to the brink over and over, but each time easing off before she fell to pieces.

Eddie could hardly stand it when Sam eventually pulled back. "*I'm* going to fuck you. Dylan, come here."

The authority in his voice flipped a switch in Eddie's brain. A haze descended, even as she mourned the loss of Dylan's fingers inside her, and she held her breath as Dylan appeared at her side, his fair, leonine form stretched out beside her, his cock digging into her thigh.

Sam looked away from Eddie and met Dylan's gaze, his eyes intense. And then he leaned forward, slowly and deliberately, and caught Dylan's lips in a sensual kiss that seemed to take Dylan by surprise. And Eddie too, as it ignited a fire in her belly that she'd never felt before. Dylan was gorgeous, and Sam was the most beautiful man she'd ever seen. Them together? Kissing? Touching?

Damn.

The kiss went on and on as Eddie watched, spellbound, as Dylan's dick responded, swelling and pulsing against her leg. And then Sam's cock jumped too, and Eddie moved on instinct, and sank down on it, taking him inside her as Sam and Dylan continued to kiss.

She rode him slowly, caught in the rhythm of his lips as they moved with Dylan's, and then hers as he broke away to kiss her too. His hips rose up to meet her gentle thrusts. He groaned into her mouth, and then broke away. "What do you want. You wanna suck Dylan too?"

In answer, she turned her head and found Dylan waiting, standing beside her, his cock at eye level, and she took him down, like she had Sam. He hit the back of her throat, and she ground down on Sam harder, revelling in his gravelly moan.

Dylan groaned too. "Shit, Eddie. You're so fucking hot. I could come from just watching you ride my boy."

Eddie sucked him deeper, gagging around his cock, and then she pulled off, and worked him with her hand as an insane bolt of reckless abandon surged through her. Dylan wasn't as big as Sam, though he was almost as beautiful. *I want them both.*

She glanced down and met Sam's heated gaze. Like he'd read her mind, her gripped her hips and thrust up into her, briefly taking control before he jerked his head to one side. "Rubbers are in the drawer."

Dylan got off the sofa-bed and moved around the room. Eddie was dimly aware of him opening a drawer in the chest by the window, but for a long moment she had eyes only for Sam as he moved inside her. And his message was clear: *Are you sure?*

God yes, she was sure. In the short time she'd known Sam, something had grown between them that would stay with her forever, but right now, in this moment, she needed more.

They all did.

Dylan came back to the bed and straddled Sam's legs. His palm was hot on Eddie's spine as he pushed her forward, and as her chest hit Sam's, her nipples grazing his heated skin, the enormity of what she was about to do—what *they* were about to do— hit her like a train.

Her eyes closed, and instinct took over. She stilled, and Sam did the same, and then Dylan pushed inside her too, his dick sliding along Sam's and filling her so entirely that she screamed out with the intensity of it.

Sam wove his fingers into her hair and yanked her head back, stealing a rough kiss as Dylan gripped her hips and fucked her—fucked them both. His thrusts were deep and steady, as measured as Sam's were fierce, but it was enough. God, it was enough, and Eddie knew that she would fall soon.

She kissed Sam over and over, flattening her body against his, absorbing his pounding heart as it kept time with hers. Her breath came in desperate gasps, and the sounds that fell from her lips seemed like they'd come from something else— some- thing wild. Primal.

And beneath her, Sam writhed too, his body an entrancing mass of beautiful tension, every tendon on his neck stretched tight. *"Eddie."*

But his warning was unnecessary, because she fell first. The coil inside her snapped, and she came hard with Sam and Dylan buried deep inside her, her body convulsing as her vision turned white. It went on and on, like she'd never stop flying. Her hands flailed, one forward to Sam's chest, and the other to wrap tight around Dylan's strong thigh.

"Fuck." Dylan dropped his weight onto Eddie. He drove into her again and again, and then he stiffened with a low ragged cry. *"Fuck."*

Beneath Eddie, Sam's gaze was fixed on Dylan, locked on his best friend as he fell apart. Sam arched from the bed, and held Eddie tight against him, pulling her down on him as he shuddered and his dick pulsed. His wet heat shot inside her and Eddie came again, another glorious wave of delirium sweeping over her until she was utterly spent.

She collapsed on Sam's chest, wine, fatigue, and satiation rendering her mute and immobile as first Dylan withdrew, and then Sam. Dylan left the sofa-bed, and Eddie heard him in the bathroom, but Sam didn't move. His breathing was deep and even, and when Eddie raised her head, his eyes were closed. She stroked his damp hair away from his forehead and kissed his cheek, and then shivered as Dylan came back into the room and did the same to her.

Eddie met his gaze, and he smiled, like the old friend Eddie knew that he—whatever happened next—was destined to become.

"Thank you," he said. "You were amazing."

TWELVE

The next morning, Eddie woke alone in Sam's bed. She sat up and surveyed the chaos of his usually tidy living space—dirty glasses and empty bottles. Rumpled sheets. A stray condom wrapper on the floor.

Eddie leaned over the side of the bed and picked it up, turning it over in her fingers as she recalled the sensation of Dylan easing inside her, fucking her and Sam both. And then she eyed the detritus of too many bottles of Polish red wine. *Good Lord, what do they put in that stuff?*

Shaking her head, she got up and wandered to the bathroom, tossing the condom wrapper in the bin as she passed. Her body was aching, and she was sore between her legs, but though she'd woken alone, the scent of both men still all around her, she felt no shame. As she turned on the shower and steam filled the spotless bathroom, exhilaration surged through her—pride, even—and she felt more like a woman than she ever had.

She was towelling her hair dry when Sam came upstairs. "I had to open up," he said. "I didn't want to wake you."

Eddie set her borrowed towel aside and turned to face him. "That's okay. I kinda figured that was where you'd gone. Did Dylan go home?"

Sam missed a beat and ran a hand through his wayward hair, tugging worriedly on it. "He left last night. Got a taxi to some bird's place in Brixton."

"We weren't enough for him, eh?"

"Um…I s'pose not."

Eddie sat on the end of the sofa-bed and looked beneath it for her clothes. Nothing. Great. She'd be walking home in the nude at this rate, but despite her preoccupation with finding her knickers, Sam's silence was deafening. She glanced up to find him still hovering in the doorway, staring at her with an expression she couldn't quite decipher. Was it regret? Eddie's heart beat too fast, and she held out her hand to him. "Is something wrong?"

Sam ventured further into the room and took Eddie's hand, sitting beside her on the sofa-bed almost absently, like his body was on autopilot. "I was going to ask you that."

"Why?"

He shrugged. "Because I've never cared about anyone me and Dylan have fucked around with before. Never woken up with them."

"Usually fuck and run?"

"Stagger off, actually. I haven't ever done that shit sober."

"Well, I've never done it all," Eddie admitted.

"Really?" Sam raised an eyebrow. "I'd never have guessed. You owned the both of us."

Eddie flushed and ducked her head. *Seriously? Now you're embarrassed?* "I honestly haven't done anything like that before, but I don't regret it, if that's what you're worried about. I know I was hammered, but I was with it enough to make my own decisions."

"I wasn't worried about that." Sam's frown melted into the devilish smirk Eddie knew so well. "As far as I recall, the whole thing was your idea."

Eddie smacked his arm. "So? I didn't hear you complaining."

Sam laughed, but then his expression sobered. "We wouldn't have laid a hand on you if you'd been off your face. Don't ever worry about that. I was freaking out more that you woke up this morning thinking me and Dylan are some kind of kinky man couple. 'Cause we ain't."

"What's wrong with being a kinky man couple?"

"Nothing. It's just not like that for us. We're *mates*."

"I know that," Eddie said. "You explained it all last night."

"Did I?" Sam rubbed his head. "I can't really remember much apart from the fuck-hot sex."

"Hanging?"

"Yeah. You?"

Eddie nodded. "It's midday and I'm still wandering around naked. What do you think?"

"I think you're hot."

The glint in Sam's eyes was nearly enough to send Eddie flat on her back, her legs wide open, begging him to fuck her again, but for once, the throbbing already going on between her legs wasn't about Sam-fuelled desire. Her body was spent, and she had no more to give.

At least not today.

"I'd better get back to work," Sam said. "You can stay if you want? I'll be done this afternoon."

"I can't," Eddie said regretfully, because the idea of

venturing out into the real world was kind of a drag. "I've got uni, and then rehearsals all evening."

"Rehearsals?"

"For the summer proms." Sam was apparently mystified. Eddie giggled and touched his cheek, smoothing away some of the lines of fatigue. "I scored a chair in the first violin section, so I'm going to be pretty busy with rehearsals until the concerts at the end of term."

"No more time for drunken threesomes, eh?"

"I'm sure I can squeeze *you* in, but no…I've got to behave myself for a few weeks. This stuff is important to me."

"I know. Me and Dylan heard you playing last night. I never realised you were so good."

"How did you— Never mind. And I'm not that good. It's taken me years to get this far. The orchestra leader is three years younger than me."

"So? Bet she can't take two dicks."

"Sam!" Eddie hit him again, but couldn't help laughing. The night she'd spent with him and Dylan might have been sordid to some, but she felt cleansed by the experience—*alive* — even with the hangover having a party in her wine-addled brain. "I've got to go."

Sam stood. "Me too. Call you later?"

Eddie smiled. "Why not?"

Sam didn't call her that night, but he was waiting outside her flat the following morning when she left for her breakfast shift at the café.

"What's this?" she asked, hoping her face didn't show how pleased she was to see him. "A personal escort?"

"As far as the café door, yes."

"You're not coming in?" Eddie had yet to make sense of the schedule Sam and his grandfather kept, and who she was working with on any particular day was a constant surprise.

"Nah, not today. I'm going to see my nan, and then I've got a hospital appointment, and then I've gotta drive Dylan to the airport."

"Hospital? Everything okay?"

Sam shrugged. "Just a check up. Pain in the arse, if you ask me."

"Keeps you healthy, though, right?"

"Uh-huh."

Eddie let it go. Since the embarrassing incident with Sam's insulin pen, she'd noticed him slipping away from time to time, and stopping in the middle of the day to eat food that he clearly didn't want. But he never talked about his diabetes. Never mentioned it. And Eddie had learned to do the same.

Sam walked her to the café, and then got in his car, disappearing into the misty morning in a haze of exhaust fumes. Eddie watched him go and imagined him screeching to a halt in front of her parents' home. *Dear Lord, it would probably finish Mum off.* Not that Eddie cared much about that. Her relationship with her mother had always been distant at best. She wondered what Sam's mother was like. He never talked about his family back in Leeds. Not even—

"You working today, missy, or what?"

Eddie sighed and turned to face Mr. Nowak. "Keep your hair on. I'm coming."

She tore herself away from the window and got down to work, and before she knew it, it was midday and time to head out. It was only as she was getting off the bus outside the orchestra rehearsal venue that she remembered that she'd neglected to ask Sam where Dylan was going.

A strange foreboding tickled Eddie's gut as she unpacked her violin and took her prized chair in the first section. *I hope he's not gone too long.*

Zurich on business. I'll be back at the end of the month xx

Eddie read Dylan's message for a third time and did the maths. The end of the month was a few weeks away, and coincided with the end of the summer term. Before her father's troubles, she'd had grand plans for three months of traveling and partying. Now, she'd be working full time at the café, giving Sam and his grandfather a taste of summer for themselves.

If she could persuade either of them to take more than one day off at a time, a feat she'd yet to accomplish.

She tapped out a reply to Dylan's message. *Wanna hang out when you get back? We still haven't had lunch.*

No reply was forthcoming, and rather than stare at a blank screen, Eddie put her phone away. And, of course, it vibrated the moment she zipped up her bag. *Every goddamn time.*

She set her violin case back on her chair and retrieved the phone from her bag, tense with anticipation, though she couldn't say why. But it wasn't Dylan, it was Sam, and the odd nerves in her belly turned to glee. *Wanna come over after work?*

As if Eddie would ever say no. As if she could. She shot back a reply—*I'll be there*—and chucked the phone in her bag. If Sam was after what she hoped he was, then she had a date with a hot shower and a razor before she was going anywhere else.

She dashed for the bus and took a seat at the back. Home was forty minutes away on this route, and she busied herself with her phone, flitting between researching the last section of her end-of-term essay, and stalking Sam and Dylan on Facebook, something she'd been meaning to do for ages. *Huh. Amazing what a job and a full course load does to your social media time.*

But the Facebook stalking turned out to be pointless. Both Sam and Dylan had meaningless profiles that they hadn't updated in months. Sam's had no activity at all, and Dylan's held only posts and photos other people—mainly girls—had tagged him in. *Typical men.*

The bus pulled up at the Vauxhall stop. Eddie jumped off and dashed for home as it began to rain. She was so intent on getting the Stradivarius inside that she didn't pay attention to the shiny Jaguar parked outside. An oversight she regretted the moment she opened her front door.

"Eddie!"

Dear God. No. "Mum? What are you doing here?"

Ellsie Dean rose from where she'd been holding court with Martha on the couch. "I came to see you, of course."

"Why?" Eddie said flatly. "You've never bothered before."

"*Edwina.* I will not have you speak to me that way. Are you not going to ask how I am?"

Yeah, 'cause it's all about you. Eddie suppressed a sigh and dumped her stuff by the coffee table, shooting Martha an apologetic wince. "Fine. How are you, Mum?"

"Well, I'd be better if your father would stop ruining every– thing. That's why I'm here—to get you to talk some sense into him."

"Sense?"

"Yes, Edwina. He came home last night and told me he's

selling the houses—all of them, and that he expects me to move into *rented* accommodation."

"Is that it?" Truth be told, Eddie was surprised the Dean family's property hadn't already been auctioned to the highest bidder. Not that she'd taken much interest, because the longer she worked at the café, saved her money, and paid her own way, the more detached she felt from the only life she'd ever known. "It's not the end of the world, Mum. Daddy's not going to put you out on the streets, is he?"

"I'd rather be on the streets than live in the house he wants to move us to. It doesn't even have a proper garage."

"You only have one car. Dad told me he's already sold the Aston and the Porsche."

"That's hardly the point."

"Then what *is* the point?" Eddie snapped. "Because if you've come here to bleat about not having enough money for your daily trip to Fortnum and Mason, you can sod right off."

"Edwina!" Eddie's mother took a step towards her. "That's enough. I know the last few months have been…difficult, but I will not have you speaking to me like that."

Eddie picked up her things, dimly aware of Martha silently fleeing the room. "Then you should've paid me a visit when this all happened. Because I'm over it now, Mum, and I really don't care how Dad's business troubles are affecting your life."

"Perhaps you'll care more when your father and I stop paying for you to live the high life in the city."

Eddie stopped on her way to her bedroom. She whirled around. "Are you fucking serious? Since when was it ever *you* and Dad paying for anything? You haven't worked a day in your life."

"Your father and I are still married, young lady. And we make financial decisions together."

Together. Eddie laughed, couldn't help it. "Mother, if that was true, then you'd know that Dad cut me off months ago. I pay my own way, in everything, even my tuition next term. Now if you don't mind, I've got shit to do. So get the fuck out of my house."

It was an hour before Eddie heard the front door finally open and close. A moment later, Martha knocked on her bedroom door. "Eddie? Are you okay? Can I come in?"

Sighing, Eddie dragged herself from her bed and opened the door. "Has she gone?"

"Yes. But she told me to tell you to buck your ideas up."

"Bitch. You should've left her to it."

"I was going to leave you *both* to it, but you flounced out before I could even shut my bedroom door, and someone had to get rid of her."

Eddie grimaced. "I'm so sorry. You've been dealing with so much of my shit lately."

Martha raised an eyebrow. "Your shit? You know you're starting to talk like Sam and Dylan, don't you?"

"How do you know what they sound like? You only spent ten minutes with them."

"More like twenty. They came in for a drink."

"A drink?" Eddie's hazy memories of that night came up blank. "Was it fun?"

"Um, yes…it was." Martha's cheeks coloured. "Well, anyway. My point is that the longer you work at the café, the more you're starting to sound like you belong there."

"And that's a bad thing?" Eddie's defensive hackles rose. "Or would it be better if I grew up to be my bloody mother?"

Martha flinched. "Actually, I was going to say that it's a good thing. Sam didn't say much the other night, but Dylan was lovely, and I had a great time at the café. So much so, that I stopped by this morning and had Sam's grandfather cook me breakfast."

"Oh." Eddie anger cooled as abruptly as it had arrived. And then came guilt…and shame, and plenty of it. "I'm sorry. I guess I just assumed you were going to say what I'd have said way back when before any of this happened. I'm so fucking sorry."

"It's okay, Eddie, honestly."

"No, it's not," Eddie insisted. "I was a dick, and that's the last thing you deserve after all you've done for me."

Martha shrugged and let it go. "I really do like the café, though. And the people. And you never told me Sam had such hot friends."

"You mean Dylan?"

"Hell yes." Martha finally ventured into Eddie's room and sat in the bed. "He was so charming too. Do you know if he's single?"

"Erm…" Eddie flailed for words. As far as she knew, Dylan was single, but Martha had never had a boyfriend, and as far as Eddie knew, was a virgin. The Dylan that Eddie knew would eat her for breakfast. "He's seeing a few people, I think. I don't know him that well."

Well enough to fuck him… Stop it.

Eddie silenced the horny devil on her shoulder and fixed Martha with the easiest smile she could manage. "Anyway, enough about me. What are you doing tonight? Do you want to go out?"

"Out?" Martha frowned. "Aren't you supposed to be saving money?"

She had Eddie there. "Okaaay, how about staying in with a DVD, some wine, and a bag of chips? On me, of course."

"Buy me a saveloy, and you're on."

Eddie giggled, but as they left the flat and raided the nearest chip shop, she realised that she couldn't remember ever doing something so ordinary with Martha. For so long, their lives had been dominated by keeping up appearances, that they'd forgotten how good the simple things were.

They sat on the sofa in their pyjamas, eating soggy chips, washed down with cheap wine, and after an hour of a tacky rom-com, both fell asleep.

THIRTEEN

For goodness *sake!*" Eddie cursed and hung up the phone as Sam's voicemail kicked in for the tenth time that morning. What the hell was he playing at?

Like you don't know…

Eddie growled and set the offending phone face down on her desk, trying to ignore the guilt and worry that had gnawed away at her since she'd woken up to a single message from Sam, asking her if she'd got lost on her way to his place the previous night.

Of course she'd replied right way, admitting that she'd drunk too much wine with Martha and fallen asleep, forgetting all about her plan to meet Sam, but she'd received no response, even though WhatsApp was telling her that Sam had read the message three hours ago.

Damn him. On any other day, Eddie would've stopped by the café, apologised in person for standing him up, all the while telling him what a prat he was for ignoring her, but that wasn't going to happen today. She had back-to-back classes, followed by a last minute cramming session for her end of term exams.

And with those exams starting in forty-eight hours, Eddie didn't have time for Sam Nowak's bruised ego.

At the front of the classroom, the lecturer stood from his desk and signalled for quiet. Eddie stifled a sigh, and put her phone on her bag. Of course, it was entirely possible that Sam was busy, rushed off his feet at the café—*and*, it wasn't like he stayed in regular contact any other day of the week—but his silence now stung.

Seriously. It wouldn't kill him to fucking acknowledge me.

And it was that indignant anger that Eddie clung to for the rest of the day, digging into it whenever she checked her phone and found that Sam still hadn't replied to her messages, or returned the dozen calls she'd made.

At the end of the day, she had half a mind to go straight home, bin off her evening shift, and shut the door on the world. But pride stopped her. It was Wednesday, the one evening of the week that she worked with Sam, and she'd be damned if she let him drive her away.

At six o'clock, she got off the bus in Vauxhall and plastered on her best nonchalant smile. She made her way to the café and breezed in like she didn't have a care in the world. But instead of a quiet café, manned only by a hopefully conciliatory Sam, she found it full of people in suits, and Mr. Nowak, with Sam nowhere to be seen.

Eddie dumped her stuff and hurried to the counter, assuming that Mr. Nowak needed help serving the bizarre influx of men who looked like they belonged in her father's office. "What's going on?" she asked. "Have they run out of teabags in Canary Wharf?"

"What?" Mr. Nowak snapped. "Don't talk in riddles at me, woman."

"I wasn't. I'm just not used to seeing so many people in here at this time of day."

Mr. Nowak merely grunted and went back to stirring his huge pots of stew. Taken aback by his surly welcome, Eddie left him without daring to ask when Sam was taking over, and went into the kitchen to fetch a box of tea-lights.

By the fridge, she found yet another suited man who was measuring the width of the kitchen. Eddie frowned, and unease prickled her skin. Sam hadn't mentioned the café having any work done, and if she remembered correctly, it had been completely refurbished a year ago. "What are you doing?"

The suited man spared her a fleeting glance. "Preparing the listing."

"The listing?" Eddie's stomach did an uncomfortable flip. "A listing for what?"

"For whatever publication my bosses choose to advertise the sale, though I don't think this place will be on the market long. It's prime real estate in this borough. This building will be high rise flats in no time."

The man went back to his business, apparently unconcerned with Eddie's deteriorating mental state as the weight of his words sank in. *Oh my God. They're selling the café.*

A cacophony of emotions hit Eddie all at once—none of them pleasant—but panic raced ahead of the outrage and sadness. She'd banked her whole summer on her job at the café…her home, and her survival at uni. And more than that, what about Sam? He'd told her often that he'd only come to London to support his grandparents. Without the café to run, would he stay?

Stop getting ahead of yourself. Mr. Nowak could be buying another place down the road for all you know. Just ask him.

Eddie took a deep breath and strode out of the kitchen, but Mr. Nowak was busy with the suits, and his stern glare kept Eddie at bay. Trying to kerb her rising anxiety, she set up the café for its regular influx of elderly diners at lightning speed, pausing only to water the clutch of spider plants at the back of the room, which was where she was when Sam finally made an appearance.

Relieved, Eddie set her watering can down and took a step forward, but Sam's answering scowl stilled her, and put the grouchy impatience she'd endured from Mr. Nowak in the shade.

Sam went straight to his grandfather and turned his back on Eddie while they talked to the men in suits. Eddie tried not to eavesdrop, but it was impossible. And the more she heard, the more horrified she became.

The suits finally left a few minutes before the café's evening clientele usually began to arrive. Mr. Nowak departed too, and Sam disappeared upstairs, leaving Eddie to greet them alone. She sat them at their favourite tables and poured wine, and then belatedly realised that she had no idea what she'd be serving them for dinner.

At the counter, peering into Mr. Nowak's huge pots and pans, she was none the wiser. If Sam didn't come down soon, she'd be forced to slop it into bowls and hope the elderly men knew their Polish peasant food better than she did.

"Put the lids back on those pan. The food will get cold."

Eddie jumped a mile. "I was just trying to figure out what it was, seeing as it seemed like I'd be serving it on my own."

"When has that ever happened? You think you're so important that we'd leave you to run the place singlehanded?"

Eddie flinched, stung by Sam's biting tone. "That's not what I meant."

"Whatever." Sam banged the lids back on the pans. "Get the plates, yeah?"

"That's all you're going to say to me?"

"What the fuck do you want me to say?"

"Um, I don't know. How about filling me on the fact that your grandfather is selling the café? That this place will be yuppie flats by the end of the summer and I'm out of a damn job?"

If Sam was surprised that Eddie knew about the impending sale of the café, he hid it well. His dark eyes flashed, and his acid glare remained. "Why would I tell you about that? It's got nothing to do with you."

"No? Gee, thanks, Sam. Way to make a girl feel special."

"You want to feel special? Is that all this is? You want the whole world to revolve around you?"

"That's not what I meant."

"Great, cos I don't actually give a shit what you meant. Pops selling the business has nothing to do with you, so either get back to work, or get the fuck out."

Sam stormed away, slamming the kitchen door behind him, and then the back door, leaving Eddie to blink away tears and wonder how a simple discussion could go so badly wrong.

She was no closer to an answer when Sam returned, smelling of rage and cigarette smoke, and apparently in no mood to continue the car crash conversation. He thrust bowls of unidentified stew at Eddie and grunted table numbers, turning away before she could respond. By the time all the customers had been served their main course, she'd about reached her limit of mutinous silence.

Furious, she stalked into the kitchen and slammed the

dish– washer closed, shoving Sam back from the counter. "No, you don't get to do this. You can't just sell the café without telling me. That's not fair."

"I told you," Sam said dully. "It's not me selling it, because it's not mine to sell. How many times do you need telling before it sinks into your entitled brain?"

"My entitled brain? Are you serious? Since when was this about your screwed up perception of me?"

"Since you made it all about you by screaming in my face about shit you know nothing about!"

Sam's shout rang out in the cramped kitchen and merged with Eddie's frustration. She pounded her fist on the stainless steel counter. "So tell me what the hell's going on. Am I out of a job, or not?"

"What do you care? You only took this job because it was the first thing you stumbled your drunk arse into. It's not like you haven't got the world at your fucking feet, even if your old man really has squandered the family millions. What does it matter to you if this place closes by the end of the month?"

"The end of the month?" Eddie's heart stuttered. "That soon?"

Sam shrugged. "If the developer the agent has in mind takes the bait, it could be even sooner. Bureaucracy works fast when the people with the real money pull the strings."

"And that's all that matters, right? Because don't tell me you haven't got a stake in this. Is that why you're pushing the sale? To get your hands on your grandfather's cash?"

It was a low blow, and she didn't mean it—how could she, when she'd seen Sam do nothing but work his fingers to the bone for his beloved grandfather?—but as Sam's molten gaze turned to ice, it was too late to take it back. He pushed past Eddie and opened the dishwasher in a cloud of steamy spray that did nothing to ease the frigid cold that had sprung up between them.

"I'm not getting shit from this sale but the chance to see Pops retire before he keels over with a fucking spatula in his hand. Now get your stuff and go home. You're done for the night."

***

"Did you give him a chance to explain why he didn't tell you?"

Eddie spun around and glared at Martha, irritated, as usual, by her insistence on being so bloody *reasonable*. After a sleepless night staring at her phone, waiting for a sign from Sam that would likely never come, she'd woken Martha at the crack of dawn in the hope of some sympathy.

But so far, none was forthcoming. Apparently there were two sides to every story—three, in this case, if you counted Mr. Nowak—and Eddie had only recounted her own.

"So?" Martha pressed. "Did Sam say why he didn't tell you about the sale?"

"Not really. He just said it was none of my business."

"Well…is it? Really, I mean, because it sounds to me like it was all only finalised yesterday. Why would he share his grand- father's business before there was something concrete for him to tell?"

"You think it's fair that I had to find out from some suit measuring up the kitchen? Or if they'd waited until they locked the damn doors for the final time?"

"It wouldn't have come to that. You said he was in a foul mood before you even spoke to him about it. Perhaps he doesn't want the café to close either? You've said yourself that his whole life revolves around it. And what about Dylan? Does he know?"

Eddie hadn't thought of Dylan any more than she'd stopped to consider Sam's real feelings. "All he said was that he wanted his grandfather to retire, and that the sale would probably happen quickly because whoever's buying it has enough money to have clout."

"Did you give him the chance to say much else?"

"Hey!" Eddie protested. "It wasn't just me ranting and raving, you know. He called me an entitled bitch."

"Seriously?"

"As good as."

"That's not the same thing, Eddie, and you know it."

Eddie sighed. "I'm wrong, aren't I?"

"To a degree, yes," Martha said. "But it sounds to me like his temper is as fiery as yours, so perhaps he said some things he shouldn't have, too. Why don't you just apologise for jumping all over him, and maybe in turn he'll tell you what's really going on?"

Martha was right, and Eddie knew it, but even after all that had passed between them, the idea of grovelling to Sam Nowak curled her fists. She left Martha to her morning and got ready for work, wondering if Sam would be in a better mood when she arrived.

But, of course, he wasn't, and he spent the whole of Eddie's shift walking away from her—leaving the kitchen whenever she came in, communicating with customers far more than he usually did in an obvious effort to keep her at bay.

And it worked, because after a sleepless night, Eddie lost the will to chase him around the café, and left at midday without saying goodbye.

FOURTEEN

The trouble with silence was that it often brought a false clarity. Eddie worked under the shadow of Sam's anger for more than a week before she finally snapped. And she was alone with her violin when the startling wave of perspective crashed into her, distracted and buzzing from nailing the climatic end of her favourite concerto. *He didn't tell me because I don't fit.*

At first, she didn't understand what that meant, and then she recalled the day she'd met Sam—how they'd faced each other in the street like two prized fighters, him sneering, and her looking down her nose. Since then, they'd worked side by side, kissed, *fucked*, and then some, but had anything really changed? From her point of view, of course it had. Her father had been right, and working at the café truly had given her the taste of the real world she'd so desperately—and unwittingly —needed. But what about Sam? Had he changed the way he saw her? *"How many times do you need telling before it sinks into your entitled brain?"* Until that moment she'd accepted the barb as words thrown out in anger, but paired with the sneer she would forever associate with him, now it *hurt.*

He looks down on me as much as I ever did on him. More.

Eddie set her violin down, fighting the sudden and terrifying urge to throw it against the wall, and wondered if Sam had experienced a similar epiphany when he'd decided not to tell her about the sale of the café. Or worse, if he'd not thought of her at all, and that made more sense than anything. After all, why would he consider someone who he thought so little of?

Far from him being a bit of rough for Eddie, she'd been the —*Oh God. I was the posh tart who dropped her knickers at the first smile.* And what about Dylan? Eddie burned as she remembered leaning forward, Sam buried deep inside her, and begging for Dylan's cock too.

With shaking hands, she packed the Stradivarius away and went to her room, her heart pounding in her chest. Dylan had never answered her message about hanging out when he got home, and she'd hardly spoken to him since *that* night. Was this why? Because he'd got all he wanted from her too?

Eddie pictured Dylan's sunny smile and shook her head. Somehow, it was easier to believe the worst of Sam than of him, even though Sam was the one who'd carved his name on her heart. She picked up her phone and scrolled through her contacts until she came to Dylan. Her thumb hovered over the delete button, but at the last second, she tossed the phone aside. And nothing changed. The weight in her chest remained. *I need to get out of here.*

Shame the only place she had to go was the café for her dinnertime shift—an evening to be spent no doubt under the cloud of Sam's mutinous silence.

And she wasn't disappointed. Sam took over from Mr. Nowak at nine o'clock and sent Eddie home half an hour later. "I don't need you," he said flatly.

"I'm aware of that," Eddie snapped. "You've made it perfectly clear."

She dropped her tea towel on the side and walked away, letting the kitchen door slam shut behind her, and wondering, as she looked at the elderly men so obliviously enjoying their supper, how long she would hold out before the bubble of grief in her belly finally burst.

She got her answer a week later when Mr. Nowak pulled a chair up to the cluster of evening tables and gave them the bad news. And even though the conversation was conducted entirely in Polish, the old men's distress was clear to see.

Unable to watch, Eddie fled into the kitchen and burst into tears. Mr. Nowak came in as she was wiping her eyes with some blue kitchen towel.

"What are you crying for? That grandson of mine forget your birthday or something?"

"What?"

"He's not one for the—how do you say it—the grand gesture? None of us Polish boys are. We show you our hearts with hard work, no?"

"I don't know what you're talking about."

"Oh." Mr. Nowak shrugged. "So it's not Sam who's upset you? You wouldn't be the first girl to be crying over my onions for that boy."

"I'll bet." Eddie sniffled and pushed the nearby bowl of sliced onions away. "But it's not Sam who's upset me...not really, anyway. It's all of you."

"All of us?" Mr. Nowak frowned. "You not get paid enough?"

"It's not about the money. It's this place...the sale. Sam never told me, and I can't help worrying about what will happen to them out there." Eddie pointed at the kitchen door. "Where will they go without you here to feed them?"

"To my friend Bolok's in Pimlico," Mr. Nowak said steadily. "You think I would shut my doors without a second thought for my friends?"

Eddie bit her lip, unwilling to admit that she had thought exactly that—assumed it, even—ever since she'd heard the news about the sale. "Did you know that before you decided to sell?"

"Of course, and I never decided to sell, Eddie. I *have* to sell, to give my Agnes the best care. Did Sam not explain this to you?"

"He didn't tell me anything," Eddie said sullenly. "Just that he was planning your retirement for you."

Mr. Nowak smiled sadly. "Ah, now that part is true. He likes to think I'll have time to be off playing poker with my friends, but that will not happen while I have my Agnes to look after. He knows this really."

"Is your wife very ill?"

"Yes, dear. She has the same as our Sam, but she is much older, and we didn't have the treatment that Sam has access to now. Her kidneys have failed, and she won't outlive them for long."

"There's nothing they can do?"

Mr. Nowak shrugged. "Perhaps, but she is old, and she's lived. She doesn't want the pain."

Eddie didn't know what to say, and in the face of real sadness, her tears dried up. "I'm sorry."

"What for? It is only because of you working here that I

have had time to see what I have to do. Now, are you done snivelling, or do I have to wash these pans on my own?"

Apparently changing the subject with a sledgehammer *was* a Nowak thing, after all. Eddie drifted to the dishwasher as Mr. Nowak left the room and opened it absently, her mind on Sam. He'd barely looked at her in a fortnight, only spared her a word when he'd absolutely had to, and it was clear that he was still as angry with her as she had been at him. He wouldn't be angry if he didn't care. But was that really true? *Could* it be true, or was Eddie's previous theory about him and Dylan the cold hard truth?

With Sam nowhere to be seen, there was no way of know‐ ing, so Eddie got back to work and spent the rest of the evening doing as much for Mr. Nowak as she possibly could.

At the end of the night, she packed up a dish of leftovers and thrust it into his hands. "You didn't eat tonight. Make sure you have these when you get home."

Mr. Nowak smiled, the harsh lines of his weathered face softening in the dim light of the empty café. "You're a good woman. Much nicer than any other girl my grandson has ever brought home."

"Been lots of them, have there?"

"A few, but none since the last one did the dirty on him a few years ago, and I was beginning to think he had given up. You're good for him, I think."

"I don't know why you think that. He hasn't spoken to me for weeks."

"He will," Mr. Nowak said. "Our boy has his mother's temperament—stubborn as a mule, no? Give him some time. He wouldn't be so cross if he didn't care."

The echo of her own hopeful thoughts set something in motion in Eddie's brain, but with back-to-back rehearsals for the end of year show packing her schedule for the next week, she didn't even have time to work at the café, let alone chase Sam around, begging him to listen to her.

And what on earth would she say? *You're as much to blame for this as I am, but please forgive me for making every assumption that you've ever accused me of?*

Yeah, right.

"For goodness sake!" Martha flicked a popcorn kernel—their dinner after a full day of rehearsals—at Eddie's head. "Just call him. I know you don't have time to go over there, but that doesn't mean you can't *talk*."

Eddie left the popcorn in her hair, too tired even to pick it out. "What if he doesn't answer?"

"Then you'll call him again until he does. He can't ignore you forever."

Eddie was willing to bet that Sam was quite capable of doing just that, and even though she'd long come around to the reality that the deadlock between them was *partly* her fault, she couldn't help being indignant that he hadn't responded to any of the handful of messages she'd sent since her last shift at the café. *Even if I'm guilty of all the things he says, I deserve a chance to explain myself.*

But did she? With Mr. Nowak's help, she'd convinced herself that Sam's anger stemmed from the fact that he really did care, but what if he didn't? What if his silence was simply the bi-product of scornful indifference?

"Eddie, you're such an overthinker."

"What?"

Martha sighed. "I can practically hear the cogs turning in your brain. Just call him, will you? Then we can all relax."

"I didn't realise it was keeping you up at night," Eddie said dryly.

"It's not, but this constant mooning over Sam is driving me up the wall. And it's ridiculous, because the café hasn't even been sold."

"It might have been, for all I know. I haven't been there for a week."

"You don't think they'd tell you?"

Eddie rolled her eyes. "Bloody hell, Martha. Don't you listen? This is how it all started. They don't tell me anything."

"No, they didn't tell you one thing. Who's to say that they haven't regretted it as much as you regret prematurely ripping Sam's head off?"

It was a nice theory, but as candid as her last conversation with Mr. Nowak had been, she couldn't imagine that she was at the top of his list of people to call when the sale of the café finally went through.

And so she got the shock of her life when her phone lit up with the café's number a few days later. Sneaking out of the orchestra pit, she answered it in a dark corridor. "Hello?"

"Hey."

"Sam?"

"Yup."

"Um…" Eddie's tongue stuck to the roof of her mouth. "Is everything okay? Do you need me to work—"

"Everything's fine. I'm calling to tell you that Pops accepted an offer on the café this morning."

"He did?"

"Yeah. It was for less than the asking price, but it was to

someone he wanted to sell it to far more than some dickhead with a corporate masterplan."

Eddie frowned. "He didn't sell it to a developer?"

"Nope. Sold it to some hipster fella who wants to serve tapas for breakfast, lunch, and dinner. And there's probably still a job for you, if you want it. They're only gonna close the place for a couple of weeks."

Eddie placed her palm over her speeding heart, and felt more than a little faint, though she couldn't tell if it was the effect that Sam's remarkably pleasant tone was having on her, or the fact that her job was apparently safe. "When will all this happen?"

"No idea. Pops wanted you to know, though, so you had time to make other arrangements if you wanted to skip out and get another job."

"Who exactly would I be skipping out on if I did that?"

"Me. The new owner offered me a job managing the place."

"What do you know about tapas?"

"Fuck all, but I don't fancy hoofing it back to Leeds any time soon, so I guess I'll learn."

"You're staying?" In all the bleak scenarios Eddie had imagined, not once had she pictured Sam staying on at the café after it was sold.

"Might as well. We didn't sell the flat, and I kinda like rolling out of bed five minutes before work."

"Jesus." Eddie leaned heavily against a nearby wall. "I thought you'd be long gone the moment the sale went through."

"I wouldn't leave my grandparents," Sam said, and then silence stretched on and on before he spoke again. "Are you still there?"

"Yes."

"Good, cos I gotta go. Pops just wanted you to have all the information so you could make decisions."

Eddie found her voice again. "That's very considerate of him. Thank him for me, will you? I know it's none of my business, so I appreciate the thought."

She hadn't meant it to sound so loaded, but even as she uttered the words, she heard the unspoken accusation, loud and clear. And apparently Sam heard it too. He chuckled coldly. "You know what, Eddie? Fuck you. If you'd come over when you said you would, I'd have told you everything. Shame you didn't show up, yeah?"

He hung up before Eddie could respond.

FIFTEEN

Oh, he didn't. Eddie stared at her phone, fury and comprehension racing through her in equal measure. So *that* was why Sam had been so angry with her. Not because she'd got up in his business and shouted in his face, but because her absence the night before had convinced him that she didn't care.

Bloody idiot, and Eddie meant that for herself as much as Sam. In all the self-inflicted drama over the sale of the café, she'd completely forgotten that she'd stood Sam up in favour of falling asleep on the couch with Martha.

Perhaps Sam would've forgotten it too, if he'd had nothing important to tell her, but that didn't mean much now. Sam was as much in the wrong as Eddie, but she couldn't deny that she'd let him down.

Her thumb moved to call him right back—apologise, call him a dick—whatever it took to heal the rift between them—but at that moment, the orchestra director summoned the string section back to work, and it was gone midnight by the time Eddie and Martha took a cab home.

Eddie didn't tell Martha about the development at the café, and when they got home, they went their separate ways. Sam remained on Eddie's mind, and she desperately wanted to call him, to hear his voice if nothing else, even if he was still angry with her, but a dawn wake-up alarm to head back to rehearsals sent her straight to bed. As much as she wanted—needed—to speak to Sam, she was so tired that she was sure she'd be asleep before he'd so much as told her to get lost.

The next morning, she cracked and called him on her way to uni. He didn't answer, and when she called the café, no one answered that phone either. Defeated, Eddie shoved her phone in her bag and forced herself to focus on the full day of rehearsals ahead.

The orchestra broke for lunch around one. Eddie checked her phone, expecting to find a blank screen. A missed call from Sam stopped her dead. She rang him straight back, but it went to voicemail.

Disappointment duelled with excitement—and more than a little apprehension. She was thrilled that he'd returned her call, but the likelihood that it was only to tell her to piss off was so high that she couldn't help wincing as she tried him again. *Just one more time.*

No luck. Voicemail again. With a world weary sigh, Eddie pocketed her phone and went back to work.

It was early evening by the time she got a chance to look again, and she'd missed two more calls from Sam. Encouraged, she rang him back, and finally—*finally*—he picked up.

"Hear me out," Eddie blurted before he could speak. "Please. Let me talk, and then you can tell me to go away."

"Go away? When have I ever been that polite?"

He had a point. Sam's choice of phrase was often far more

colourful, but the fact that he was taking the piss out of her gave her hope that perhaps he really was willing to listen.

She took a deep breath. "I'm sorry."

"What for?"

"Everything—for standing you up, not listening, raging, making assumptions about your life when I had no place to do so, even after I'd learned not to."

"That's all, eh?"

"Well, I suppose I could swing for more, but I'd rather just tell you how I feel."

"Why?"

"Why what?"

"Why do you want to tell me how you feel? Why does it matter?"

Eddie sighed heavily. "I don't know, Sam. It just does, okay? It all matters to me, and it always did. I didn't mean to stand you up. I passed out on the couch with Martha, and then I forgot, and then all this…*shit* happened at the café, and everything fell apart."

"I thought you were fucking that greasy stiff from the city."

"What? Ian? Why on earth would you think that?"

Silence, and then Sam's sigh echoed Eddie's. "Cos in my experience, when most girls stop showing up for dates they're usually boning someone else."

"I'm not most girls, Sam. And I don't *bone* anyone."

Sam chuckled, though he suddenly sounded profoundly tired. "Oh I know that, and I probably always did, but it took Pops ripping me a new one this afternoon to make me really see it."

"What's your grandfather got to do with this?"

"He likes you better than he likes me," Sam said dryly.

Eddie smiled, and warmth spread through her blood, soothing her rehearsal-weary bones. "You'd never tell."

"No? You think he makes a habit of hauling damsels in distress off the street and giving them a job?"

Eddie had no answer to that. She picked up her violin case and left the orchestra pit, making her way to the entrance hall. She found a seat in a quiet corner and slumped, throwing her feet up on a nearby table.

It felt odd to relax her body so much while her brain and heart were working a million miles an hour, but she went with it—had to—because everything that truly mattered seemed to depend on this conversation.

Dramatic, much? But it was true. Sam *mattered,* even if he was as much of an arsehole now as he'd always been. *I don't hate him anymore.*

"Eddie? You there?"

"Sorry, what?"

"You went all silent on me."

"Not nice, is it?" Eddie quipped before she could stop herself, but Sam merely chuckled, reminding her that this was how their dynamic worked when they actually communicated — a healthy mix of banter, sarcasm, and heady sexual tension.

"So..." he said. "What?"

"I'm still waiting for you to tell me how you feel."

"I feel like I want to kiss you."

"That it?"

"No, there's more." Eddie crossed her legs and considered how she truly felt at that precise moment. "I feel like I want to see you more—outside of work, I mean—and hold you, and be there for you, and do all the things you're probably going to say you don't need or want."

"What makes you think I don't need those things?"

"Because you're a stubborn arsehole."

"So are you, but you need those things too, right?"

A few months ago, Eddie would've disagreed, but though she'd only had a taste of how those things could be with Sam, she wanted more…she wanted it *all*. "I want to be with you."

Silence, and then Sam sighed. "I'm not very nice, Eddie. And I've got nothing to offer you that you haven't seen already. Waiting tables, frying eggs…partying at a dirty metal club—it's pretty much all I've got."

"And you don't think that's enough? You think you're less of a man than some city lawyer or banker?"

"No, I don't think that. But you might, deep down."

"That's not fair."

"Isn't it? Eddie, you don't know any better."

The resignation in Sam's tone made Eddie sit up. She planted her booted feet on the floor and shook her head, even though Sam couldn't see her. "You might've been right a few months ago, but not now. I see *you*, Sam. And it's you that I want."

"Not Dylan? He's more your type than me—nice, successful, business trips abroad and all that shizzle."

It was hard to tell if Sam was joking, so Eddie answered the question honestly. "I like Dylan, and I liked fucking him, but it's not him I think of when I'm alone every night. Not him that I'd give anything to touch right now, and I couldn't give a toss what either of you do for a living."

"I wish I could see you."

Sam's voice was husky, and Eddie closed her eyes, the tension in her shoulders easing slightly. "I wish I could see you too, but I've got rehearsals all day tomorrow, and Friday, before the first concert in the evening."

"And then you're playing all weekend?"

"Yes…hey, why don't you come to opening night? I have a family ticket going spare. I was going to give it to Martha for her brother, but he's not coming."

"What about your family?" "They're not coming either."

"Why not?"

"My dad's busy, and my mum's a self-centred bitch, so I told her to fuck off. That's kinda where I was when I stood you up. She showed up at the flat in the afternoon."

Eddie didn't add that her invitation to her father had bounced back with an "out of office" email. Or that her single phone call to him had, like most of Sam's, gone unanswered.

And Sam let it go. "Just tell me where to be, and I'll be there."

Eddie fiddled nervously with the hem of her borrowed dress. In years gone by, she'd gone all out and bought herself at least two brand new outfits to choose from before each end of year concert, but there'd been no money for that this year, and she was glad of it. Martha's black lace fit like a dream, and left her plenty of time to worry about things that actually mattered.

Like Sam, and if he'd managed to pick up the ticket she'd left him at the door. For the millionth time, Eddie cursed the orchestra director who'd decreed that phones were banned from pit on performance days. Eddie hadn't spoken to Sam all day, and she was getting twitchy.

What if he doesn't show?

Strike the getting. She *was* twitchy. Because Sam showing up tonight felt like a commitment to so much more—even

Dylan seemed to think so now that his phone had finally found some service. *"He's stressing about what to wear, Eddie. What the fuck have you done to my boy?"*

"He's my boy now." Eddie had teased back, but was that really true? Could Sam be tamed? Did he even want to be? If he didn't show tonight, Eddie reckoned not.

"He'll be here," Martha murmured, appearing at Eddie's side like a ghost. "Stop fretting."

"I'm not."

"Liar."

Eddie poked her tongue out at turned away. She'd filled Martha in on all that was Sam—including the sale of the café—on the way home the night before, and Martha had been suitably excited. And ridiculous. *"I knew he loved you."*

He doesn't love me. Of that, Eddie was certain, though she couldn't deny that she was perilously close to loving him.

"Places, please!"

The orchestra director called the musicians to the pit. Eddie filed out with the first violin section and took her seat, feeling the swell of anticipation as the choir followed suit on the stage above. The audience couldn't see them yet, but it wouldn't be long, and Eddie wondered if she'd be able to concentrate knowing that Sam was watching. Aside from that one night at the café—the one that had led to her falling into bed with him and Dylan both—he'd never heard her play.

Until now.

The curtain rose. Eddie felt the heat of a thousand eyes on her and a prickle at the back of her neck. Was that Sam? The ticket hadn't had a seat number on it, so he could be anywhere— front or back. A few feet away from her if he'd got there nice and early.

Eddie didn't dare look, sensing that a glimpse of Sam would be enough to fritz her focus, because it had always been that way with him—his scent, his broad shoulders, the thralldom of his molten gaze. It was a wonder Eddie had made the first section at all with Sam Nowak in her life.

The concert played out, and it was flawless. *Eddie* was flaw- less, even in the fleeting solo that she'd been given at the last minute. She drew her bow across the strings a final time, basking in the cloud of resin, her eyes fixed on the conductor, and then it was over. Thunderous applause filled the venue, and the orchestra rose as one. Eddie finally looked out over the crowd, searching, her chest full to bursting with pride, excitement…and love. *Where are you?*

But she couldn't see Sam, and she tried not to be disappointed as the orchestra left the stage. There were a thousand people in the audience. She'd find Sam outside, by the oak tree, where he'd agreed to meet her after if she didn't find him first.

Eddie packed the Stradivarius away at record speed and fled the rowdy staging area. She hurried outside to the courtyard and scanned the milling audience members for any sign of Sam. There was none, so she ran to the oak tree by the gates, but he wasn't there either. A call to his phone went straight to voice- mail, and the longer Eddie stood alone beneath that damn fucking tree, the clearer her reality became.

Sam wasn't there.

There were no words to describe the bone crushing disappointment Eddie felt as she rode the bus back to Vauxhall.

Sam's phone remained turned off, and her messages went unanswered. He hadn't showed, and Eddie reckoned she knew why. As the bus rolled into her stop, she fired off a final text. *Thanks for not showing up. Message received, loud and clear.*

There was no reply, but she didn't expect one. It was obvious that Sam had decided that he didn't belong in her world, or him in hers, and he wasn't interested in proving himself wrong. *Well, fuck you, Sam Nowak. My world matters as much as yours.*

Eddie got off the bus and went straight home, bypassing her usual route past the café. At the flat, she chucked her phone on the floor and threw herself onto her bed, fully intent on spending the rest of the night tossing and turning, and silently telling Sam Nowak just where he could shove his job at the new café.

But of course, she fell asleep, and her mind was blissfully blank until an insistent noise from her phone woke her sometime later.

Stumbling in the dark, she lurched, chest first, out of bed and grabbed it, answering the call without looking at the screen. "Hello?"

"Eddie? You awake?"

"Dylan?" Eddie hauled the rest of her body out of bed, tripped over the dress she'd fallen asleep in, and landed in a heap on the floor. "What's up?"

"Is Sam with you?"

Eddie snorted. "No. Why would he be with me?"

"Because of the concert. I assumed you guys would go home together."

"Well, you assumed wrong. He didn't show up." Sleep-addled as she was, Eddie fought hard to keep the bitterness from her voice.

She lost. Not that Dylan seemed to notice. "What do you mean, he didn't show up? Did he call?"

"No, Dylan. He didn't call. And he didn't answer when I called him, so *I'm* going to assume that he had a better offer. That all right with you?"

"He wouldn't just not show up."

"Of course he would," Eddie retorted. "I was an idiot to think he'd be interested in coming in the first place."

"Nah, it wasn't like that. He was chuffed that you'd asked him."

Eddie took a breath to argue, but the worry in Dylan's tone stopped her short. "What are you trying to say? Do you think something's wrong?"

"I don't know, but he hasn't answered his phone all day, and now it's off, and I can't reach Artur either."

"Artur would've gone home by now. He closes the café earlier than Sam." Eddie rubbed her eyes and scrambled to her feet. "And he knows Sam's supposed to be with me tonight, so he wouldn't think to check on him."

Shit. Eddie had noticed from the beginning how Mr. Nowak often popped his head upstairs in the evening, just to check that Sam was okay. Always called the café when he wasn't working. Just to *check*. Dear God, why hadn't Eddie done the same? "I'm going over there."

"Good. Listen, Eddie, I might be really fucking wrong about this—I have been before—and if I am, you have my blessing to barge in there and punch him in the face, but if I'm not, you need to call me immediately, okay? I'll tell you what to do."

"Okay. I'll call." Eddie grabbed a pair of nearby boots and yanked them on, tearing her stockings with her thumbnail.

"Wait, though. If he doesn't answer the door, how am I going to get in? The café's closed."

"The alleyway," Dylan said. "And don't bother knocking. Just go up the metal stairs and get the key from behind the gas metre. That'll get you into the landing, and you know where the flat key is, right?"

"With the napkins."

After promising again to call Dylan back as soon as possible, Eddie hung up and dashed out of her bedroom, swiping her coat and keys from where she'd dumped them on the coffee table, and charging out into the night. It had begun to rain while she'd slept, that heavy, muggy summer rain that left huge puddles in every indent of the pavement.

Eddie ran through them, splashing dirty water up her legs, and raced the five hundred metres or so between her flat and the café. On any other night, the pitch dark alleyway would've given her pause for thought, but she ignored the danger and hurried through until she reached a small yard she'd only ever seen through the storeroom window.

She pounded the metal steps with her boots and retrieved the key from the gas metre cupboard. Inside, she knocked over the box of napkins, scattering packets everywhere.

Frantic, as she was now painfully certain that Dylan was right, she tossed them aside as she searched for the second key. *Gotcha!* She snatched the Judas Priest keyring and stuck the single key in the lock, kicking the door open and shouldering her way inside.

The door swung shut behind her, cloaking her in darkness. The flat was quiet and still, and at first not a thing seemed out of place. Eddie glanced around, taking in the folded sofa-bed with its neat stack of blankets, the clear coffee table, and spotless kitchen area. She poked her head in the bathroom and found it empty.

Feeling somewhat calmer, she turned back to the living room, and then she saw him, and her heart stopped dead. "Sam?"

SIXTEEN

Eddie dashed into the kitchen and dropped to Sam's side where he was slumped against a cupboard door. "Sam? *Sam?*"

Sam groaned and clumsily swiped at her chest, but then he fell slack again, his eyes closed, disappearing into the pallor of his cold, clammy skin.

Eddie shook him. "Sam!"

But there was no response, and with her stomach in her throat, she somehow found her phone and called Dylan. "Something's wrong."

"Is he conscious? Breathing?"

"He's breathing, but I can't wake him up. He's passed out on the kitchen floor."

"Okay, I need you to listen very carefully and do exactly as I say."

"Why? What's wrong? Should I call an ambulance?" "Maybe, but you need to treat him first. He needs medication, and he needs it fast."

"His insulin?"

"No! God, no. Not that. It'll make him worse. Eddie, I

need you to listen. First, you need to put him in the recovery position. Can you do that?"

Eddie considered Sam's slumped form and tried to picture the recovery position from the handful of first aid lessons she'd had at school. "I think so."

"Do it, carefully. And don't take any notice if he tries to stop you. If he comes round at all, he won't have a clue what's going on."

But Sam didn't come round as Eddie manoeuvred him onto his side. He didn't react at all, and the fear roaring in Eddie's ears was a savage beast. She stroked Sam's hair out of his face. "I'm here. It's okay."

"Eddie?" Dylan's voice was sharp with worry. "Did you do it?"

"Yes."

"Good. Now, I need you to open the drawer by the fridge. Inside, you'll find a glucagon kit."

"A what?"

"Trust me, you'll see it."

Eddie scrambled to her feet and opened the drawer, wedging her phone under her chin. Inside, there was nothing but a red plastic case. She grabbed it and pried it open to find a vial and a syringe. "Is it an injection kit?"

"Yes. You need to set it up, and inject it into Sam. Can you do that? Because if you can't, we need to call an ambulance right now."

"I can do it. Just tell me how."

"Break the seal on the glucagon powder and take the case off the syringe."

Eddie obeyed. "Done. What now?"

"Stick the needle into the rubber stopper on the powder vial and inject the stuff in the syringe into it. Done it?"

"Yes."

"Good, now shake it until it's clear. It's gotta be clear, or you can't use it."

"Okay. Clear. Got it." Eddie shook the vial, eyes trained on the cloudy liquid until it cleared. "It's done."

"Right, now you need to stick the needle back in and suck it all up into the syringe, then you need to inject it into Sam."

"Where? Where do I inject him?"

"His arm, his leg, whatever. Suck up the glucagon first. Make sure you get it all."

Eddie stuck the needle into the rubber stopper on the vial and drew back the plunger on the syringe, sucking up all of the clear liquid. Then she slowly withdrew the needle and stared between it and Sam, nausea rushing up her throat. "Which part of his arm?"

"His bicep is fine. Push his sleeve up and put your thumb where you want to inject."

"Done."

"Okay, now get a wipe from the needle case and quickly clean the injection site."

"Damn it, Dylan. Couldn't you have told me that before? I've got my hands full." Eddie let go of Sam's arm and stretched back, snagging the red case that she'd carelessly discarded. She snatched a wipe and tore it open with her teeth, and rubbed it over Sam's skin. "There. Clean. Do I inject him now?"

"Yes, but be careful. Only push the plunger down, don't draw it up again. Oh, and wait until the needle's all the way in before you do anything else, okay?"

Eddie was far from okay, but adrenaline saved her focus. She brought the needle to Sam's skin and pushed it in, then she pressed the plunger down until all of the glucagon solution had disappeared into Sam's body. "It's in. Now what do I do?"

"Pull the needle out, slowly, then apply pressure to the site."

"With what?"

"I don't know. His fucking T-shirt. Anything."

Eddie withdrew the needle and pressed the sleeve of Sam's T-shirt to the tiny wound. A micro-speck of blood seeped through, and she shivered. She knew shamefully little about Sam's illness, and she couldn't imagine what it must be like to live in a body that regularly tried to kill you. "How long will it take to work?"

"Not long. If he doesn't come round in five minutes, you'll need to call that ambulance, okay?"

"I shouldn't call it now?"

"I think it's safe to wait now he's had the glucagon. The paramedics will probably want to take him in, and he gets a bit shitty about being manhandled."

"Unless it's you, right?"

Dylan chuckled tensely. "Trust me, he prefers you. Is he moving yet?"

"No."

"Don't worry. It'll happen, but can you do something while you wait?"

"Sure."

"Go into the hall and open the wardrobe by the door. At the bottom there's a cardboard box with a couple of spare glucagon kits in it. Get one, and stick it in the drawer."

"For next time?" Eddie got up and followed Dylan's instructions, her phone still wedged tightly under her chin. "So we know where it is?"

"Exactly. You saved his life with that injection. He'd have died if you hadn't found him."

The enormity of what had just happened hit Eddie like a train. Dazed, she drifted back to the kitchen and shoved the glucagon kit in the drawer. She hadn't saved Sam. Dylan had, because if it hadn't been for him, she'd have slept the night away while Sam was dying on his kitchen floor.

A strangled sob escaped her.

"Eddie…" Dylan said softly. "It's not your fault. I only knew because I've been through it with him before. I only caught it the first time by accident."

"What if he doesn't wake up?"

"He will."

And as Dylan spoke, Sam stirred at Eddie's feet. Phone forgotten as it clattered to the floor, she dropped to her knees. "Hey. Can you hear me?"

Sam brought his arms beneath him and tried to push himself up, but he didn't have the strength, and Eddie caught him as he collapsed back down, tugging him gently into her lap. "I've got you," she whispered. "I've got you."

A low, pained sound escaped Sam, and somehow, he found Eddie's hand, though she couldn't tell if he knew that it was hers. She squeezed it tight and put her lips to his ear, whispering, "I've got you" over and over until he finally opened his eyes. Eddie released Sam's hand and cupped his face in her open palms, wiping his watery eyes with her thumbs. "Sam? You okay?"

Sam blinked a few times before recognition dawned in his bloodshot eyes. "Eddie?"

"It's me. I'm here. Are you all right?"

"Um…" Sam swallowed. "Need sugar. Need food."

"Okay…hang on a sec." Eddie stretched over Sam and

grabbed her phone, praying that Dylan was still there. "He's awake. He wants sugar. Can he have it? Is that the right thing to do?"

"Yes." The relief in Dylan's voice was clear. "In the cupboard next to the sink, you'll find Lucozade, honey, and stuff like that. If he can sit up and drink, give him the Lucozade. He'll know how much to take. Once the sugar starts to work, he'll need some real food. After that, put him to bed, and stay with him, checking his sugar levels every hour for the next five hours. If you're worried, call an ambulance."

Eddie frowned, struggling to absorb the influx of information. "Where are *you* going?"

"Nowhere you can't reach me. Can Sam talk? Put him on, if he can."

Eddie held the phone to Sam's ear. "It's Dylan. He wants to talk to you."

Sam nodded, and closed his eyes as Dylan spoke to him, then he nodded again and grinned slightly. "Dickhead."

Eddie took that as her cue to reclaim her phone, and when she looked at the screen, Dylan had gone. Which meant she was on her own. *Sugar. He needs sugar.* "Sam? I need to get to the cupboard. Can you sit up?"

Not on his own, apparently, but between them they managed to get Sam sitting up enough for Eddie to wriggle out from beneath him and retrieve the Lucozade from the cupboard. She held it to his lips and helped him drink, and it worked fast, and before long he was apparently determined to get up.

"I'm supposed to put you to bed," Eddie protested.

"So do it." Sam climbed unsteadily to his feet, his face still deathly pale. "I could do with lying on something soft."

Eddie couldn't argue with that. She left Sam holding himself up on the kitchen counter and hurried to the living room to open the sofa-bed. With that done, she fetched the pillows and duvet she knew he left in the airing cupboard, and set up the bed.

Sam had made his way to the living room doorway by the time she was done. "You don't have to do that. I'd have been fine on the couch."

"Get in the bed," Eddie said absently, distracted by a sudden and horrific thought. *My God, how long was he unconscious?* "Sam?"

"Yeah?"

"How long were you on the floor?"

Sam said nothing as he carefully got himself to the relative safety of the sofa-bed. "I don't know, to be honest. I can never remember much if I have a really fucked up hypo."

"Hypo?"

"Yeah, that's what happens if my blood sugar drops too low. Sometimes I can catch it with some food, like we did the other week, remember? But I didn't get home in time and I couldn't fix it."

"Why didn't you call someone?"

Sam shrugged. "I don't know. I can't remember coming home—oh *shit*."

"What is it?" Eddie flew instantly to his side. "What is it? What's the matter?"

Sam hung his head and covered his face with his hands. "Your concert. I missed it, didn't I?"

Oh Sam. Eddie wrapped her arms around him and held him close. "It doesn't matter. You can come to the next one."

Sam sighed heavily and pressed his face against Eddie's

chest. His reply was muffled, and Eddie let him be, trusting that he'd repeat it when she could bear to let him go.

Which wasn't happening anytime soon, though it was clear that Sam needed to lie down. She coerced him into bed, and lay with him, holding him and stroking his hair, while she considered if he'd have anything in his fridge that she could make for him. Considering the war chest Dylan had directed her to in the cupboard, she assumed so, but assumption had got her in trouble of late.

She nudged Sam gently, rousing him from his daze. "Dylan says you need to eat. Have you got anything in, or do I need to raid the café?"

A ghost of grin warmed Sam's tired face. "There's food in the fridge, I ain't Mother Hubbard, you know."

Giggling, Eddie forced herself to let him go and got out of bed, kicking her abandoned boots into the corner so they wouldn't clutter up Sam's ordered home too much. In the fridge, she found an Aladdin's cave of Polish leftovers and her stomach growled, reminding her that she hadn't eaten either. She grabbed potato pancakes, cold sausages, cheese, and the sauerkraut she'd become addicted to, and chucked it on a plate.

Sam was sitting up when she got back to bed, and her choice of midnight snacks seemed to amuse him. "You like the Polish food, eh?"

Eddie shrugged. "Your grandfather has fed me enough of it, it's hard not to. Now stop taking the piss and eat up."

For once Sam did as he was told, and the more he ate, the more colour came back to his cheeks. And Eddie ate too, and felt the fear-laced adrenaline finally fade, though the guilt remained. *I'd never have forgiven myself if—*

But she couldn't complete the thought, and the pancake in her mouth turned to dust.

She pushed the plate at Sam. "Finish that. I need to use your bathroom."

"Eddie—"

"It's okay," she said. "I just need a moment."

She fled the room before Sam could protest and locked herself in the bathroom, splashing cold water on her face. The frigid shock did little to ease her jittery heart or shaky hands, but it did serve to clear her mind enough for her to realise that her private pity party was kind of pathetic. *It's not you who spent God-knows how long on the kitchen floor.*

With a heavy sigh, she washed her hands and returned to the living room. The dirty plate had somehow found its way to the kitchen, though Sam didn't appear to have moved. "You better not have washed it."

Sam said nothing, just shifted over to make room for her, but he caught her arm before she could slide in beside him. "Have my T-shirt. You can't sleep in that dress."

That he wasn't trying to get her naked was telling. Eddie helped Sam out of his T-shirt, then raised up on her knees to shimmy her borrowed dress over her head. Sam's T-shirt smelled amazing, and felt better against her skin than any dress ever could.

"Do you feel better?" she asked when they were huddled down again.

"Yeah. I'll be fine by the morning."

Eddie wasn't convinced, and now that Sam was bare-chested, the sight of the tiny red welt on his arm reminded her of Dylan's other instructions. "How do you check your blood sugar?"

"Hmm?" Sam opened his eyes. "Oh, fuck…yeah. Hang on."

He rolled over and reached for the coffee table that Eddie had shoved aside when she'd unfolded the bed. On it was the bag Sam often left lying around the café. He retrieved it and lay down again, unzipping it to reveal his insulin pen and what Eddie presumed was a device to test his blood sugar levels.

The process turned out to be relatively simple, and apparently painless, though Eddie couldn't help wincing as the tiny drop of blood oozed from Sam's finger. And the numbers meant nothing to her. "Is that good or bad?"

"Better," Sam said. "Give me a couple of hours and I'll be right as rain."

"Do you need to eat anything else?"

"Nah, I'm good till breakfast. You're staying, right?"

Eddie pushed Sam onto his back and leaned over him, pressing her chest against his, counting the steady beat of his heart. "I'm not going *anywhere.*"

Eddie woke to warm hands roaming her body, and soft kisses on the back of her neck. Still mostly asleep, her body naturally arched, pushing her against Sam's hard cock as it dug into her spine.

"I know you're awake," he whispered. "Roll over so I can see you."

Eddie obeyed without question, and when she met Sam's gaze, her heart leapt. Clear and bright, it was the most beautiful sight she'd ever seen. "You're back."

"I was never gone."

Eddie begged to differ, but as Sam tugged her borrowed T-shirt over her head, words seemed unnecessary. She arched up into him and shivered as her breasts brushed his warm skin. Her legs naturally fell open for him, cradling him between her thighs, but then she looked up at him, and remembered that just a few hours ago, he'd been unconscious on the kitchen floor.

She moved fast and toppled Sam onto his back, straddling him before he could protest. And the fact that he let her gave away that perhaps he wasn't feeling as sharp as he claimed. Eddie pressed her forehead to his and stared into his eyes, losing herself, all the while searching for any sign of the terrifying vacancy she'd witnessed the night before. "Are you okay?"

"Never better."

"Liar."

Sam started to roll his eyes, then seemed to think better of it. "How about I lie here good as gold and let you take care of me?"

Eddie grinned. "I think I can live with that."

She moved her lips to his and kissed him, lightly at first, but then deeper, harder, as she undulated her hips on top of him, grinding a slow circle that made her wet. Sam seemed to like it too. He broke away from Eddie's kiss to savage her neck, drag- ging his teeth over her sensitive skin, and his groans met her gasps with every roll of her hips.

For a while, it was a perfect cadence, but then the need for more overwhelmed Eddie. She wriggled out of her underwear and tossed it aside, then moved down Sam's body, relieving him of the sweatpants he'd slept in.

On her way back up, his cock was too tempting to ignore. She took him in her mouth and teased him with a gentle suction, grazing him with her teeth, shuddering when his hips bucked in response, and his hands found their way to her messy hair.

He wove his fingers into the tangled strands and tugged just hard enough for the answering shot of pain to be wonderfully pleasurable. "If you want me to shoot in your mouth, you're going the right way about it."

Already? Eddie smirked around Sam's dick. That was a new one. Usually he had her on a knife edge before she'd truly realised what he was doing to her. Having the upper hand now felt odd—good, but strange, like it was happening to someone else.

Sam pulled her off him, gently forcing her to look at him. "Fuck me."

Eddie didn't need asking twice. She crawled up over him and kissed him again, her body instinctively aligning with his, and then she sank down him oh-so-slowly, taking him in, inch by inch, her breath coming in stuttered pants as she watched his eyes widen, and then roll, and then flutter closed.

"Dear God, woman. You're gonna kill me before anything else does."

That suited Eddie just fine, in the metaphorical sense, of course. She fucked Sam at a snail's pace, driving them both to near madness, until his thumb found its way to her clit, and she shattered into a million pieces.

Sam came with a quiet groan that sounded almost pained. When perspective returned to Eddie, she raised her head and quickly took his face in her sweaty palms. "Are you okay? Did I hurt you?"

"Nah. I'm good, baby."

Eddie shook him gently. "You sure? What time is it, anyway? We need to check your blood sugar."

Sam sighed. "Is this how it's gonna be from now on? You fucking the living shit out of me, then turning into my mother before my dick's out of you?"

"Ew. You're so crude."

"Yup. It's a valid concern, though."

"It is today, and maybe tomorrow," Eddie admitted. "You scared me."

"I'm sorry."

"Well, you shouldn't be. If anyone should be sorry, it's me."

"How'd you figure that shit?"

"Because if I hadn't been such a pigheaded—"

Sam silenced Eddie with a fierce kiss. "Fuck that. I've spent the last four years trying to convince Dylan he's not responsible for this shit. I can't start all over again with you. This is *my* problem. Always has been. Don't treat me like a fucking invalid, and don't blame yourself when I conk out on you."

Eddie pulled her face away from him and scowled. "Are you done?"

"Only if you were really listening, because I'm kinda certain that you won't let me tell you how fucking sorry *I* am for missing your performance."

"Well, you're right about that, at least," Eddie conceded. "It was hardly your fault."

"Yes and no. I missed lunch because I forgot to get my jacket from the dry cleaners. And then I burned my only shirt with the iron and went out to get a new one without checking my sugars." Sam looked away. "I know better than that."

She caught his chin and forced him to look at her. "Then we've both been morons these past few days, haven't we? Good job we have each other."

"I'll say." Real humour finally pierced the troubled haze that had descended over Sam's beautiful face. "Without me you'd still be screwing toffs in tweed."

"And you'd still be—oh wait…doing who, Sam? Because Dylan told me you were going through a dry spell."

It was a playful fib, and Eddie wasn't altogether sure she even wanted to know what Sam had been up to before she'd come along. Unless it involved Dylan, of course, and—

"You have such a dirty mind."

Eddie blushed, and couldn't deny that Sam had caught her red-handed, even if he couldn't possibly know the exact place her Sam-fuelled imagination had taken her. She slid off him and pressed herself into his side. "Shut up and check your blood sugar."

"Yeah, yeah."

Sam's grumble was fierce and earnest, but for the first time since Eddie had met him, he kissed her cheek and did as he was bloody told.

SEVENTEEN

The last end of year performance was held at the Royal Albert Hall. Last year, her parents had driven into the capital in their Bentley and sat in the private boxes, even though she'd been at the back of the second violin section. Her mother had held court at the cocktail reception after, and for one night only, Eddie had felt like her parents truly loved her—that she wasn't a mere accessory to a lifestyle she'd eventually come to realise was as hollow as her father's smile.

This year, her parents didn't come, and Eddie had never felt prouder as she took her final bow from the first section, and looked through the crowd to see Sam right at the back with Mr. Nowak, both men applauding louder than anyone else, their faces alive with genuine love and affection.

Eddie's face hurt as she beamed at them, and she waved too, not giving a crap about protocol. Sam's answering smile was blinding, and as hard as she'd worked to gain an early promotion in the orchestra, as many hours as she'd lost preparing for this moment—for all of that, she couldn't wait to get off stage and ditch this place.

Because there would be no stuffy cocktail parties for Eddie tonight. Lord, no. Sam was meeting her outside, and as soon as they'd dropped Mr. Nowak home, they were hitting the town— *Sam's* town—and Eddie couldn't wait. She hurried off stage and packed the Stradivarius away, passing it, as ever, to Martha for safekeeping.

Martha hugged her. "Have fun. I wish I was coming with you."

"You still can. Screw the Ritz."

"If only. Sometimes I wish my parents would set me free like yours. You're so happy, Eddie. I can't help being jealous."

Martha spoke with a wry smile, but Eddie took her words to heart. Free. Happy. Was that what she was? Was that how she *felt?* As she left the orchestra behind and dashed out to the brightly lit city street, straight into Sam's open arms, the warmth that enveloped her—inside and out—didn't seem too far off the mark.

Sam lifted her off her feet. "Did you slay it?"

"I tried." Eddie planted a kiss on his lips, remembering to keep it demure for Mr. Nowak's sake. "Did you enjoy it?"

Sam winced. "I think so? It ain't no Five Finger Death Punch, but I love watching you play. You know that."

Eddie *did* know that. In the last few weeks, Sam had come to every concert and recital he was able to, and rarely a day passed when he didn't badger her to play for him in private. *I'm so lucky.* She kissed him again, then wriggled free so she could see Mr. Nowak. "What about you, Artur? Did you enjoy it?"

"Yes, Yes." Mr. Nowak clapped Eddie on the back, his large hand dwarfing her slender shoulder. "I liked the sprightly one after the interval. We used to dance to music like that when I was a boy. You must come to the house and play it for me again some time."

"You know the rules," Eddie quipped. "Feed me first."

"Woman, you're worse than a teenage boy."

Mr. Nowak released her and set off to where Sam's car was parked down the road. Eddie started to follow him, but Sam tugged her back. "Are you sure you want to go out tonight? We can just go home if you're tired?"

"Screw that," Eddie protested. "You've endured all my stuffy orchestra functions. I wanna come rocking with you."

Sam chuckled. "Fair enough. I've got your boots in the car. Do you need anything else from your place?"

"Nope. I'm good."

Sam eyes Eddie's full length lace dress. "Sure about that?"

"I'm sure. Let's go."

They caught up with Mr. Nowak at the car and took him home. Then they drove back to Vauxhall and ditched Sam's car at the café. Sam poked his head in to check that Dylan had closed down properly, and Eddie took advantage of his absence to fix her outfit.

She kicked her high heels into the boot of Sam's car and stamped into the battered Doc Marten's she'd bought off eBay for the occasion. Then, after taking a furtive glance around, set about ripping the skirt of her dress away until it was six inches above her knees. She made a few holes in her stockings too, then fished lipstick and eyeliner out of her bag. Black kohl and bright red lips completed her look, and she stepped back from the car's wing mirror with a satisfied smile. Punky-goth wasn't a look she'd dabbled in before, but the vampy colours suited her pale skin, and she hoped Sam thought so—

A wolf whistle cut into her thoughts. she whirled around to find Sam leaning on the wall behind her, his eyebrows raised in appreciation. "You're gonna be fighting them off tonight."

"You're not going to fight them off for me?"

"You don't need my help telling the world what you want."

Sam pushed off the wall and stepped into Eddie's personal space. "Though I'd obviously batter any fucker who didn't listen."

"Obviously." Eddie rolled her eyes to cover her shudder. Sam didn't have much of a tough guy act, but then he didn't need one. Eddie had seen much bigger men instinctively move out of his way. "Are you ready to go?"

"Lead the way."

Eddie took Sam's hand, and they walked a few streets until the thrum of Sam's favourite metal club began to buzz through the pavement. A shot of nerves ran through Eddie. She'd been looking forward to this—to exploring a new side of Sam—for days, but the age-old fear that she just wouldn't fit was some- times as present as it had ever been since Sam had stormed into her life three months ago.

Sensing, as always, the subtle shift in her mood, Sam stopped walking and abruptly took her in his arms, sweeping her off her feet, and spinning in a long, slow circle.

Eddie giggled and threw her head back. Sam could be a man of few words—especially pleasant ones—but in moments like these, platitudes were unnecessary. *I love him.* It was true, though she'd yet to find the balls to tell him.

Sam set her down and they continued to the club. The bouncers at the door waved Sam inside like they knew him well, and Eddie stuck close to him as they passed through the entrance—a cool, blue-lit alcove—and into the main club.

And then the music hit her, loud and raw, and heady smoke filled her senses, and she knew in a pounding heartbeat why this club was Sam's home from home whenever time allowed. *God*, the music. Far from the tuneless roar she'd expected, the electric riffs, speeding drums, and throbbing bass seeped into her soul as much as Sam had, and she was suddenly and instantly lost.

Hand in hand with Sam, she followed the music to the stage where a band of what looked like renegade lorry drivers was tearing the place up. All of them fascinated her, but the bass player captivated her most of all—the way his jaw moved with every throbbing note, and the belying speed of his huge fingers as they danced up and down the frets.

"See something you like?" Sam murmured in her ear. "You've got that look in your eye."

"What look?"

"The one you get when you're jabbering on about Vaughan Williams."

Eddie tore her eyes from the stage, surprised that Sam had remembered her late night rant about her second shot at a Lark Ascending solo.

"I do not jabber."

"I've got a sleepless night says otherwise."

Sam had given Eddie her fair share of sleepless nights, but she let it slide. It had been a fortnight since she'd found him on his kitchen floor, well on his way to a hypoglycaemic coma —*thanks for the education, Dylan*—and after a day or so of rest, he'd bounced back so well it was hard to imagine that it had happened at all. Shame her brain remembered every moment of that night in such painful detail that her imagination was rendered redundant.

"*Eddie*…listen to the music, baby." Sam grabbed her around the waist and pulled her close, spinning her away from the stage as he moved her with the music, his hips grinding into her with every brutal dig of the bass guitar. "That's what we came for, remember? To loosen you up a little."

Eddie glared up at him, even though the humour in his gaze was obvious. "You want me to loosen up? Maybe we should find Dylan and ask him to join us?"

"If you want."

Sam's expression gave nothing away, but Eddie cracked first, and shook her head. Their night with Dylan had been incredible, and a repeat performance was definitely *not* out of the question, but for now, her heart craved only Sam.

They lost themselves to the heat and noise of the club, slow- dancing and kissing, getting slowly drunk on bottles of warm lager. It was nearly dawn when they stumbled out. Habit drew them to the café, stopping at a dodgy kiosk on the way for some hot chips stuffed into a ketchup-laced pita bread. Eddie had never eaten such a thing, but fast realised that it was the food of the Gods.

The drunk Gods, at least.

Back at Sam's flat, he hustled Eddie into the shower. "Trust me, you'll appreciate it in the morning when you don't wake up smelling of grime and chip fat."

"I wasn't about to protest being naked in an enclosed space with you."

"No? Good. 'Cause I've been dreaming about ripping your clothes off all night."

"Have at it." Eddie spread her arms wide. "They're ruined anyway."

As if Sam needed asking twice. He tore her clothes from her body and pushed her under the hot spray, placing her hands on the tiled wall, and bending her over. And then he fucked her, holding her hair back from her face, and curving his body behind her, moulding himself to her, as he brought her to an orgasm that rocked her equilibrium to the point where it was only his strong hands that kept her upright.

She fell slack against him and closed her eyes. "*Sam.*"

"Don't worry," he whispered. "I've got you."

"Eddie?"

Sam stirred, his arm clumsily reaching for her, and she smiled, catching his hand before he could reclaim it and go back to sleep. *Bless him.* She'd noticed this in the nights they'd spent together since he'd been ill—the way he'd say her name and reach for her long before he was even awake.

Sometimes, she found herself wondering whose name he'd uttered before her, but other times, like now, she found that she didn't care. Sam had made no verbal commitment to her, but something had changed between them in the last few weeks... grown, and solidified. And even if he didn't feel for her like she did for him, nothing that had come before mattered. How could it, when it was only his touch that had brought her to life?

Sam shifted again, effectively dumping his head in her lap, which was apparently his favourite place to be, in any context. Eddie rubbed her fingers absently through his hair and turned her attention back to the window, lost again in the cloudless sky she'd been staring at since she'd woken an hour ago to the thrum of the café below.

Today was Mr. Nowak's last shift before Sam shoved him unceremoniously toward a retirement he didn't want. After that, Sam and Eddie would be running the place alone until the new owner took over, and after that? Who knew? Sam had agreed to stay on and run the café, but how he'd deal with someone else calling the shots remained to be seen. Sam was unconcerned. Eddie? Not so much. *He'll deck someone within a week.*

"Shh."

Eddie glanced down. Sam gazed back at her. Somehow she'd missed him waking up and lacing his fingers with hers. "Morning. What are you shushing me for? I didn't say anything."

Sam stretched, his gorgeous chest arching from Eddie's lap. "You don't have to when your brain is having a party like that."

Eddie rolled her eyes and huffed. "Why do people always say that to me?"

"Because you've got the worst poker face in the world."

"That right?"

"Yup."

"Okay, hotshot. So what am I thinking about then, if I'm so bloody transparent?"

Sam sat up, the covers slipping down his body and reminding her that he was as naked as she was. "You're wondering what the fuck you're doing here."

"Here?"

"Yeah, shacked up in this grotty flat when you could've woken up bathed in gold."

"What the hell are you talking about?"

"You know what I'm talking about." Sam reached down the side of the sofa-bed and retrieved his blood sugar test kit. "And it's okay. I look at you all the time and wonder why you want to be here."

He drew blood from his finger and studied the tiny monitor. A figure flashed up, but it meant nothing to Eddie. She was still learning what magic numbers meant that Sam was well.

She waited for him to put the kit away. Then chose her words carefully. "Sam, I want to be here because you make me happy."

Or not so carefully. Embarrassed, she looked away, but Sam caught her chin in his strong hand. "But why? I've got nothing for you. If you want shit loads of money, you'll have to go out and get it yourself."

"Even if I wanted that, what would be wrong with earning it myself? Do you think I want to be like my mother? So fucking dependent on the rest of the world that I don't know how to put petrol in my own car?"

"I don't know what you want. I'm not a mind reader."

"What?"

Sam shrugged. "I want to be with you—at work, at home, in bed, but I haven't got a clue how you feel."

"*You* don't know how *I* feel?" Eddie blinked, unsure if she'd heard right.

"How the hell would I? It ain't like you make a point of telling me, unless you've got the hump, then the whole world bloody knows—"

Eddie pounced on him, half furious and half delirious that the door to his heart she'd sought all this time finally appeared to be open. She kissed him fiercely, smothering his surprised grunt, and tumbling him onto his back before he inevitably regained control.

He caught her arms and flipped her, covering her with his body, pinning her down. "Something I said?"

Eddie grinned. "All this time I've been wondering what the hell you're doing with a prissy brat like me."

"You're not prissy."

"I am a brat, though."

"No more than I am. Is there a point to this?"

"There is now." Eddie kissed him again, gentler this time, less intent on knocking his teeth out, before she sobered enough to explain herself. "I guess I just need to know if you're serious about…well, me, I suppose. My life's changed so much, but I've honestly never been happier. I just need to know that it's real."

Sam licked his lips, and for a fleeting moment looked as though he'd deflect Eddie's unspoken question with what had brought them together in the first place, but then he smiled, and his molten eyes shone. "I don't know what that hell goes on between you and me sometimes, but I can tell you one thing: it's fucking real. I, uh, I can't remember what my life was like without you."

"Really?"

Sam nodded slowly. "Yeah, and some days I don't know if that's a good or a bad thing, because I'm not used to giving a shit, you know? It scares me."

Eddie could believe that. Outside of his family, Dylan, and now her, Sam didn't seem to care much about anything. "The way I feel about you scares me too, but it's a good fear, Sam. I'd miss it if it wasn't there."

"I'd miss *you*, if you weren't around. Is that enough?"

Eddie honestly didn't know, but for now it would have to be.

They got up and meandered, bleary eyed, downstairs to the café for breakfast. A carnival atmosphere greeted them, as it seemed that every Polish immigrant in London had turned out to wish Mr. Nowak well.

"We should give them a hand," Sam said, gesturing to Mr. Nowak and Dylan, who were rushed off their feet.

But Mr. Nowak wouldn't hear of it. "Not today, Sammy. Today, I cook for you, and you watch. Be your last chance to learn something, eh?"

And apparently that included Eddie too. Mr. Nowak hustled them to the last free table and plied them with enough breakfast to see them through the week. They were just finishing up when Dylan stopped by the table and dropped a kiss on Eddie's cheek. "Want me to kiss him too?"

"Piss off." Eddie shoved him away. "You two are never going to let me forget that night, are you?"

Dylan laughed. "Not if we can help it. But what's so bad about that? Sam loves you. I love fucking you. Winners all round, if you ask me."

Eddie choked on the dregs of her tea. "Sam doesn't love me."

"Says who?" Sam snapped.

She looked at him. "Says *you*…or, at least, you've never told me otherwise, which is the same thing."

"No, it isn't."

"On that note…" Dylan got up from where he'd stooped to kiss Eddie. "I'm gonna leave you to it, but Sam?"

"What?"

Dylan ignored the growl in Sam's voice and flashed a winning smile. "Just tell her, man. Don't be a dick about it."

He sauntered away, leaving Eddie to glare at Sam, eyebrow raised, fists clenched. "*That's* how I get to find out that you love me? You couldn't just *fucking* tell me?"

Sam's scowl faded. "Where would be the fun in that?"

"This isn't a bloody game." Eddie pushed back her chair, elation and hurt warring in the pit of her stomach. She loved Sam too, more than she could ever say, but she didn't want to live like this, playing games over a plate of egg on toast. She wanted Sam to love her, to respect her, and to be proud for the world to know it. She wanted—

Sam grabbed her hands and yanked her out of her seat. "I know it's not a game. I'm just shit at saying stuff, okay? You know this, and if you love me back, we're gonna have to learn to work with it. And that's a big if, cos the last time I checked, you weren't throwing around the declarations either. So what's it gonna be? Do you love me, or not? Because I *love* you, and if you don't feel the same, we're wasting our fucking time anyway."

"I love you, Sam."

"Yeah? Then why the fuck didn't *you* say—"

It was the second time that day that Eddie had silenced him with an earth-moving kiss, but the difference this time was that they weren't alone—they weren't holed up in his flat, naked in bed. They were in the café, yards away from where their story had begun, and as the crowd of Polish regulars catcalled and whistled, Eddie knew that whatever happened from this moment on, she'd found her home.

DYLAN

In case you're wondering, Dylan does get his love story. Catch up with him (and Sam and Eddie) in my MM novel Dream.

NEWSLETTER

For the most up to date news and free books, subscribe to my newsletter HERE.

This is a zero spam zone. Maximum number of emails you will receive is one per month.

PATREON

Not ready to let go of Sam, Eddie, and Dylan? Or looking for sneak peeks at future books in the series? Alternative POVs, outtakes, and missing moments from **all** Garrett's books can be found on her Patreon site. Misfits, Slide, Strays...the works. Because you know what? Garrett wasn't ready to let her boys go either.

Pledges start from as little as $2, and all content is available at the lowest tier.

And PS: There's lots of Dylan on my Patreon site.

ABOUT THE AUTHOR

Bonus Material available for all books on Garrett's Patreon account. Includes short stories from Misfits, Slide, Strays, What Remains, Dream, and much more. Sign up here: https://www.patreon.com/garrettleigh

Facebook Fan Group, Garrett's Den... https://www.facebook.com/groups/garre...

Garrett Leigh is an award-winning British writer, cover artist, and book designer. Her debut novel, Slide, won Best Bisexual Debut at the 2014 Rainbow Book Awards, and her polyamorous novel, Misfits was a finalist in the 2016 LAMBDA awards, and was again a finalist in 2017 with Rented Heart.

In 2017, she won the EPIC award in contemporary romance with her military novel, Between Ghosts, and the contemporary romance category in the Bisexual Book Awards with her novel What Remains.

When not writing, Garrett can generally be found procrastinating on Twitter, cooking up a storm, or sitting on her behind doing as little as possible, all the while shouting at her menagerie of children and animals and attempting to tame her unruly and wonderful FOX.

Garrett is also an award winning cover artist, taking the silver medal at the Benjamin Franklin Book Awards in 2016. She designs for various publishing houses and independent authors at blackjazzdesign.com, and co-owns the specialist stock site moonstockphotography.com

Connect with Garrett
www.garrettleigh.com